All of the raw power he projected was clearly—and safely—locked down.

He turned her hand over and kissed the back of it. In the enclosed space of the office, with no one to witness his chivalrous gesture, she couldn't tell if the kiss was a threat or a seduction. Or both.

Then he raised his gaze and looked her in the eyes. Suddenly, the room was much warmer, the air much thinner. Frances had to use every ounce of her self-control not to start taking huge, gulping breaths just to get some oxygen into her body. Oh, but he had nice eyes, warm and determined and completely focused on her.

She might have underestimated him. "I'm not going to take the job."

He laughed then. It was a warm sound, full of humor and honesty. It made her want to smile.

"I wasn't going to offer it to you again. You're right—it is beneath you."

Here it came—the trap he was waiting to spring. He leaned forward, his gaze intent on hers.

"I don't want to hire you. I want to marry you."

* * *

Falling for Her Fake Fiancé is part of the Beaumont Heirs series: One Colorado family, limitless scandal!

Dear Reader,

Welcome back to Colorado! The Beaumont Heirs are one of Denver's oldest, most preeminent families. They are the children of Hardwick Beaumont. Although he's been dead for almost a decade, Hardwick's womanizing ways—the four marriages and divorces, the ten children and uncounted illegitimate children—are still leaving ripples in the Beaumont family.

Frances Beaumont is the fifth heir and the first daughter. Frances learned early that a woman of beauty and connections was in high demand, and she has both. But she's made a series of risky investments just as the family business was sold off. Suddenly, she's broke and out of favor. She wants things to go back to the way they were—when the Beaumont name commanded respect and money.

Ethan Logan is the new CEO of the Beaumont Brewery. He's discovered that replacing a Beaumont is no easy task. He can't control the workers, and unless something changes he'll lose control of the company. So when Frances strolls into his office with *his* employees falling all over themselves to help her, he sees a way to regain control—he proposes. It's when Frances says yes that the real games begin!

Falling for Her Fake Fiancé is a sensual story about accepting your past and embracing the future. I hope you enjoy reading this book as much as I enjoyed writing it! For more information about the other Beaumont Heirs, be sure to stop by www.sarahmanderson.com and sign up for my newsletter at http://eepurl.com/nv39b!

Sarah

FALLING FOR HER
FAKE FIANCÉ

SARAH M. ANDERSON

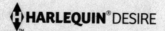

Recycling programs
for this product may
not exist in your area.

ISBN-13: 978-0-373-73418-4

Falling for Her Fake Fiancé

This edition published by arrangement with Harlequin Books S.A.

For questions and comments about the quality of this book, please contact us at CustomerService@Harlequin.com.

® and TM are trademarks of Harlequin Enterprises Limited or its corporate affiliates. Trademarks indicated with ® are registered in the United States Patent and Trademark Office, the Canadian Intellectual Property Office and in other countries.

Printed in U.S.A.

Award-winning author **Sarah M. Anderson** may live east of the Mississippi River, but her heart lies out West on the Great Plains. With a lifelong love of horses and two history teachers for parents, she had plenty of encouragement to learn everything she could about the tribes of the Great Plains.

When she started writing, it wasn't long before her characters found themselves out in South Dakota among the Lakota Sioux. She loves to put people from two different worlds into new situations and to see how their backgrounds and cultures take them someplace they never thought they'd go.

Sarah's book *A Man of Privilege* won the 2012 RT Reviewers' Choice Award for Best Harlequin Desire. Her book *Straddling the Line* was named Best Harlequin Desire of 2013 by *CataRomance*, and *Mystic Cowboy* was a 2014 Booksellers' Best Award finalist in the Single Title category as well as a finalist for the Gayle Wilson Award of Excellence.

When not helping out at her son's school or walking her rescue dogs, Sarah spends her days having conversations with imaginary cowboys and American Indians, all of which is surprisingly well tolerated by her wonderful husband. Readers can find out more about Sarah's love of cowboys and Indians at sarahmanderson.com.

Books by Sarah M. Anderson

HARLEQUIN DESIRE

The Nanny Plan

The Bolton Brothers

Straddling the Line
Bringing Home the Bachelor
Expecting a Bolton Baby

The Beaumont Heirs

Not the Boss's Baby
Tempted by a Cowboy
A Beaumont Christmas
His Son, Her Secret
Falling for His Fake Fiancé

Visit the Author Profile page at Harlequin.com, or sarahmanderson.com, for more titles.

To Jennifer Porter, who took me under her wing before I was published and helped give me a platform to talk about heroes in cowboy hats. Thank you so much for supporting me! We'll always have dessert at Junior's together!

One

"*Mis*-ter Logan," the old-fashioned intercom rasped on Ethan's desk.

He scowled at the thing and at the way his current secretary insisted on hissing his name. "Yes, Delores?" He'd never been in an office that required an intercom. It felt as if he'd walked into the 1970s.

Of course, that was probably how old the intercom was. After all, Ethan was sitting in the headquarters of the Beaumont Brewery. This room—complete with hand-carved everything—probably hadn't been redecorated since, well...

A very long time ago. The Beaumont Brewery was 160 years old, after all.

"*Mis*-ter Logan," Delores rasped again, her dislike for him palatable. "We're going to have to stop production on the Mountain Cold and Mountain Cold Light lines."

"What? Why?" Logan demanded. The last thing he could afford was another shutdown.

Ethan had been running this company for almost three months now. His firm, Corporate Restructuring Services, had beat out some heavy hitters for the right to handle the reorganization of the Beaumont Brewery, and Ethan had to make this count. If he—and, by extension, CRS—could turn this aging, antique company into a modern-day business, their reputation in the business world would be cemented.

Ethan had expected some resistance. It was only natural. He'd restructured thirteen companies before taking the helm of Beaumont Brewery. Each company had emerged from the reorganization process leaner, meaner and more competitive in a global economy. Everyone won when that happened.

Yes, thirteen success stories.

Yet nothing had prepared him for the Beaumont Brewery.

"There's a flu going around," Delores said. "Sixty-five workers are home sick, the poor dears."

A flu. Wasn't that just a laugh and a half? Last week, it'd been a cold that had knocked out forty-seven employees. And the week before, after a mass food poisoning, fifty-four people hadn't been able to make it in.

Ethan was no idiot. He'd cut the employees a little slack the first two times, trying to earn their trust. But now it was time to lay down the law.

"Fire every single person who called in sick today."

There was a satisfying pause on the other end of the intercom, and, for a moment, Ethan felt a surge of victory.

The victorious surge was short-lived, however.

"*Mis*-ter Logan," Delores began. "Regretfully, it seems that the HR personnel in charge of processing terminations are out sick today."

"Of course they are," he snapped. He fought the urge to throw the intercom across the room, but that was an impulsive, juvenile thing to do, and Ethan was not impulsive or juvenile. Not anymore.

So, as unsatisfying as it was, he merely shut off the intercom and glared at his office door.

He needed a better plan.

He always had a plan when he went into a business.

His method was proven. He could turn a flailing business around in as little as six months.

But this? The Beaumont freaking Brewery?

That was the problem, he decided. Everyone—the press, the public, their customers and especially the employees—still thought of this as the Beaumont Brewery. Sure, the business had been under Beaumont management for a good century and a half. That was the reason All-Bev, the conglomerate that had hired CRS to handle this reorganization, had chosen to keep the Beaumont name a part of the Brewery—the name-recognition value was through the roof.

But it wasn't the Beaumont family's brewery anymore. They had been forced out months ago. And the sooner the employees realized that, the better.

He looked around the office. It was beautiful, heavy with history and power.

He'd heard that the conference table had been custom-made. It was so big and heavy that it'd been built in the actual office—they might have to take a wall out to remove it. Tucked in the far corner by a large coffee table was a grouping of two leather club chairs and a matching leather love seat. The coffee table was supposedly made of one of the original wagon wheels that Phillipe Beaumont had used when he'd crossed the Great Plains with a team of Percheron draft horses back in the 1880s.

The only signs of the current decade were the flat-screen television that hung over the sitting area and the electronics on the desk, which had been made to match the conference table.

The entire room screamed Beaumont so loudly he was practically deafened by it.

He flipped on the hated intercom again. "Delores."

"Yes, *Mis*—"

He cut her off before she could mangle his name again.

"I want to redo the office. I want all this stuff gone. The curtains, the woodwork—and the conference table. All of it." Some of these pieces—hand carved and well cared for, like the bar—would probably fetch a pretty penny. "Sell it off."

There was another satisfying pause.

"Yes, sir." For a moment, he thought she sounded subdued—cowed. As if she couldn't believe he would really dismantle the heart of the Beaumont Brewery. But then she added, "I know just the appraiser to call," in a tone that sounded…smug?

He ignored her and went back to his computer. Two lines shut down was not acceptable. If either line didn't pull double shifts tomorrow, he wouldn't wait for HR to terminate employees. He'd do it himself.

After all, he was the boss here. What he said went.

And that included the furniture.

Frances Beaumont slammed her bedroom door behind her and flopped down on her bed. Another rejection—she couldn't fall much lower.

She was tired of this. She'd been forced to move back into the Beaumont mansion after her last project had failed so spectacularly that she'd had to give up her luxury condo in downtown Denver. She'd even been forced to sell most of her designer wardrobe.

The idea—digital art ownership and crowdsourcing art patronage online by having buyers buy stock in digital art—had been fundamentally sound. Art might be timeless, but art production and collection had to evolve. She'd sunk a considerable portion of her fortune into Art Digitale, as well as every single penny she'd gotten from the sale of the Beaumont Brewery.

What an epic, crushing mistake. After months of delays and false starts—and huge bills—Art Digitale had been live for three weeks before the funds ran out. Not a single transaction had taken place on the website. In her gilded life, she'd never experienced such complete failure. How could she? She was a Beaumont.

Her business failure was bad enough. But worse? She couldn't get a job. It was as if being a Beaumont suddenly counted for nothing. Her first employer, the owner of Galerie Solaria, hadn't exactly jumped at the chance to have Frances come back, even though Frances knew how to flatter the wealthy, art-focused patrons and massage the delicate egos of artists. She knew how to sell art—didn't that count for something?

Plus, she was a *Beaumont*. A few years ago, people would have jumped at the chance to be associated with one of the founding families of Denver. Frances had been an in-demand woman.

"Where did I go wrong?" she asked her ceiling.

Unsurprisingly, it didn't have an answer.

She'd just turned thirty. She was broke and had moved back in with her family—her brother Chadwick and his family, plus assorted Beaumonts from her father's other marriages.

She shuddered in horror.

When the family still owned the Brewery, the Beaumont name had meant something. *Frances* had meant something. But ever since that part of her life had been sold, she'd been…adrift.

If only there was some way to go back, to put the Brewery under the family's control again.

Yes, she thought bitterly, that was definitely an option. Her older brothers Chadwick and Matthew had walked away and started their own brewery, Percheron Drafts. Phillip, her favorite older brother, the one who had gotten her into parties and helped her build her reputation as the Cool Girl of Denver high society, had ensconced himself out on the Beaumont Farm and gotten sober. No more parties with him. And her twin brother, Byron, was starting a new restaurant.

Everyone else was moving forward, pairing off. And Frances was stuck back in her childhood room, alone.

Not that she believed a man would solve any of her problems. She'd grown up watching her father burn through marriage after unhappy marriage. No, she knew love didn't exist. Or if it did, it wasn't in the cards for her.

She was on her own here.

She opened up a message from her friend Becky and stared at the picture of a shuttered storefront. She and Becky had worked together at Galerie Solaria. Becky had no famous last name and no social connections, but she knew art and had a snarky sense of humor that cut through the bull. More to the point, Becky treated Frances like she was a real person, not just a special Beaumont snowflake. They had been friends ever since.

Becky had a proposition. She wanted to open a new gallery, one that would merge the new-media art forms with the standard classics that wealthy patrons preferred. It wasn't as avant-garde as Frances's digital art business had been, but it was a good bridge between the two worlds.

The only problem was Frances did not have the money to invest. She wished to God she did. She could co-own and comanage the gallery. It wouldn't bring in big bucks, but it could get her out of the mansion. It could get her back to being a somebody. And not just any somebody. She could go back to being Frances Beaumont—popular, respected, *envied*.

She dropped her phone onto the bed in defeat. *Right.* Another fortune was just going to fall into her lap and she'd be in demand. *Sure.* And she would also sprout wings.

True despair was sinking in when her phone rang. She

answered it without even looking at the screen. "Hello?" she said morosely.

"Frances? Frannie," the woman said. "I know you may not remember me—I'm Delores Hahn. I used to work in accounting at—"

The name rang a bell, an older woman who wore her hair in a tight bun. "Oh! Delores! Yes, you were at the Brewery. How are you?"

The only people besides her siblings who called her Frannie were the longtime employees of the Beaumont Brewery. They were her second family—or at least, they had been.

"We've been better," Delores said. "Listen, I have a proposal for you. I know you've got those fancy art degrees."

In the safety of her room, Frances blushed. After today's rejections, she didn't feel particularly fancy. "What kind of proposal?" Maybe her luck was about to change. Maybe this proposal would come with a paycheck.

"Well," Delores went on in a whisper, "the new CEO that AllBev brought in?"

Frances scowled. "What about him? Failing miserably, I hope."

"Sadly," Delores said in a not-sad-at-all voice, "there's been an epidemic of Brew Flu going around. We had to halt production on two lines today."

Frances couldn't hold back the laugh that burst forth from her. "Oh, that's fabulous."

"It was," Delores agreed. "But it made Logan—that's the new CEO—so mad that he decided to rip out your father's office."

Frances would have laughed again, except for one little detail. "He's going to destroy Daddy's office? He wouldn't dare!"

"He told me to sell it off. All of it—the table, the bar,

everything. I think he'd even perform an exorcism, if he thought it'd help," she added.

Her father's office. Technically, it had most recently been Chadwick's office. But Frances had never stopped thinking of her father and that office together. "So what's your proposal?"

"Well," Delores said, her voice dropping past whisper and straight into conspirator. "I thought you could come do the appraisals. Who knows—you might be able to line up buyers for some of it."

"And..." Frances swallowed. The following was a crass question, but desperate times and all that. "And would this Logan fellow pay for the appraisal? If I sold the furniture myself—" say, to a certain sentimental older brother who'd been the CEO for almost ten years "—would I get a commission?"

"I don't see why not."

Frances tried to see the downside of this situation, but nothing popped up. Delores was right—if anyone had the connections to sell off her family's furniture, it'd be Frances.

Plus, if she could get a foothold back in the Brewery, she might be able to help all those poor, flu-stricken workers. She wasn't so naive to think that she could get a conglomerate like AllBev to sell the company back to the family, but...

She might be able to make this Logan's life a little more difficult. She might be able to exact a little revenge. After all—the sale of the Brewery had been when her luck had turned sour. And if she could get paid to do all of that?

"Let's say Friday, shall we?" That was only two days away, but that would give her plenty of time to plan and execute her trap. "I'll bring the donuts."

Delores actually giggled. "I was hoping you'd say that."

Oh, yes. This was going to be great.

* * *

"*Mis*-ter Logan, the appraiser is here."

Ethan set down the head count rolls he'd been studying. Next week, he was reducing the workforce by 15 percent. People with one or more "illness absences" were going to be the first to find themselves out on the sidewalk with nothing more than a box of their possessions.

"Good. Send him in."

But no nerdy-looking art geek walked into the office. Ethan waited and then switched the intercom back on. Before he could ask Delores the question, though, he heard a lot of people talking—and laughing?

It sounded as though someone was having a party in the reception area.

What the hell?

He strode across the room and threw open his office door. There was, point of fact, a party going on outside. Workers he'd only caught glimpses of before were all crowded around Delores's desk, donuts in their hands and sappy smiles on their faces.

"What's going on out here?" he thundered. "This is a business, people, not a—"

Then the crowd parted, and he saw her.

God, how had he missed her? A woman with a stunning mane of flame-red hair sat on the edge of Delores's desk. Her body was covered by an emerald-green gown that clung to every curve like a lover's hands. His fingers itched to trace the line of her bare shoulders.

She was not an employee. That much was clear.

She was, however, holding a box of donuts.

The good-natured hum he'd heard on the intercom died away. The smiles disappeared, and people edged away from him.

"What is this?" he demanded. The color drained out

of several employees' faces, but his tone didn't appear to have the slightest impact on the woman in the green gown.

His eyes were drawn to her back, to the way her ass looked sitting on the edge of the desk. Slowly—so slowly it almost hurt him—she turned and looked at him over her shoulder.

He might have intimidated the workers. He clearly had not intimidated her.

She batted her eyelashes as a cryptic smile danced across her deep red lips. "Why, it's Donut Friday."

Ethan glared at her. "What?"

She pivoted, bringing more of her profile into view. *Dear God, that dress—that body.* The strapless dress came to a deep V over her chest, doing everything in its power to highlight the pale, creamy skin of her décolletage.

He shouldn't stare. He *wasn't* staring. Really.

Her posture shifted. It was like watching a dancer arrange herself before launching into a series of gravity-defying pirouettes. "You must be new here," the woman said in a pitying tone. "It's Friday. That's the day I bring donuts."

Individually, he understood each word and every implication of her tone and movement. But together? "Donut Friday?" He'd been here for months, and this was the first time he'd heard anything about donuts.

"Yes," she said. She held out the box. "I bring everyone a donut. Would you like the last one? I'm afraid all I have left is a plain."

"And who are you, if I may ask?"

"Oh, you may." She lowered her chin and looked up at him through her lashes. She was simply the most beautiful woman he'd ever seen, which was more than enough to turn his head. But the fact that she was playing him for the fool—and they both knew it?

There were snickers from the far-too-large audience as

she held out her hand for him—not to shake, no. She held it out as though she expected him to kiss it, as if she were the queen or something.

"I'm Frances Beaumont. I'm here to appraise the antiques."

Two

Oh, this *was* fun.

"Donut?" she asked again, holding out the box. She kept as much innocence as she could physically manage on her face.

"You're the *appraiser*?"

She let the donut box hang in the space between them a few more moments before she slowly lowered the box back to her lap.

She'd been bringing donuts in on Fridays since—well, since as long as she could remember. It'd been her favorite part of the week, mostly because it was the only time she ever got to be with her father, just the two of them. For a few glorious hours every Friday morning, she was Daddy's Little Girl. No older brothers taking up all his time. No new wives or babies demanding his attention. Just Hardwick Beaumont and his little girl, Frannie.

And what was more, she got to visit all the grown-ups—including many of the same employees who were watching this exchange between her and Logan with rapt fascination—and hear how nice she was, how pretty she looked in that dress, what a sweetheart she was. The people who'd been working for the Brewery for the past thirty years had made her feel special and loved. They'd been her second family. Even after Hardwick had died and regular Donut

Fridays had faded away, she'd still taken the time to stop in at least once a month. Donuts—hand-delivered with a smile and a compliment—made the world a better place.

If she could repay her family's loyal employees by humiliating a tyrant of an outsider, then that was the very least she could do.

Logan's mouth opened and closed before he ordered, "Get back to work."

No one moved.

She turned back to the crowd to hide her victorious smile. They weren't listening to him. They were waiting on her.

"Well," she said graciously, unable to keep the wicked glint out of her eye. Just so long as Logan didn't see it. "It has been simply wonderful to see everyone again. I know I've missed you—we all have in the Beaumont family. I do hope that I can come back for another Donut Friday again soon?"

Behind her, Logan made a choking noise.

But in front of her, the employees nodded and grinned. A few of them winked in silent support.

"Have a wonderful day, everyone," she cooed as she waved.

The crowd began to break up. A few people dared to brave what was no doubt Logan's murderous glare to come close enough to murmur their thanks or ask that she pass along their greetings to Chadwick or Matthew. She smiled and beamed and patted shoulders and promised that she'd tell her brothers exactly what everyone had said, word for word.

The whole time she felt Logan's rage rolling off him in waves, buffeting against her back. He was no doubt trying to kill her with looks alone. It wouldn't work. She had the upper hand here, and they both knew it.

Finally, there was only one employee left. "Delores,"

Frances said in her nicest voice, "if Mr. Logan doesn't want his donut—" She pivoted and held the box out to him again.

Oh, yes—she had the advantage here. He could go right on trying to glare her to death, but it wouldn't change the fact that the entire administrative staff of the Brewery had ignored his direct order and listened to hers. That feeling of power—of importance—coursed through her body. God, it felt *good*.

"I do not," he snarled.

"Would you be a dear and take care of this for me?" Frances finished, handing the box to Delores.

"Of course, Ms. Frances." Delores gave Frances a look that was at least as good as—if not better than—an actual hug, then shuffled off in the direction of the break room, leaving Frances alone with one deeply pissed-off CEO. She crossed her legs at the ankle and leaned toward him, but she didn't say anything else. The ball was firmly in his court now. The only question was did he know how to play the game?

The moment stretched. Frances took advantage of the silence to appraise her prey. This Logan fellow was *quite* an attractive specimen. He was maybe only a few inches taller than Frances, but he had the kind of rock-solid build that suggested he'd once been a defensive linebacker—and an effective one at that. His suit—a very good suit, with conservative lines—had been tailored to accommodate his wide shoulders. Given the girth of his neck, she'd put money on his shirts being made-to-order. Bespoke shirts and suits were not cheap.

He had a square jaw—all the squarer right now, given how he was grinding his teeth—and light brown hair that was close cut. He was probably incredibly good-looking when he wasn't scowling.

He was attempting to regain his composure, she realized. Couldn't have that.

Back when she'd been a little girl, she'd sat on this very desk, kicking her little legs as she held the donut box for everyone. Back then, it'd been cute to hop down off the desk when all the donuts were gone and twirl in her pretty dress.

But what was cute at five didn't cut it at thirty. No hopping. Still, she had to get off this desk.

So she extended her left leg—which conveniently was the side where one of the few designer dresses she'd hung on to was slit up to her thigh—and slowly shifted her weight onto it.

Logan's gaze cut to her bare leg as the fabric fell away.

She leaned forward as she brought her other foot down. The slit in the dress closed back over her leg, but Logan's eyes went right where she expected them to—her generous cleavage.

In no great hurry, she stood, her shoulders back and her chin up. "Shall we?" she asked in a regal tone. "My cloak," she added, motioning with her chin toward where she'd removed the matching cape that went with this dress.

Without waiting for an answer from him, she strode into his office as if she owned it. Which she once had, sort of.

The room looked exactly as she remembered it. Frances sighed in relief—it was all still here. She used to color on the wagon wheel table while she waited for the rest of the workers to get in so she could hand out the donuts. She'd played dolls on the big conference table. And her father's desk…

The only time her daddy hugged her was in this room. Hardwick Beaumont had not been a hard-driven, ruthless executive in those small moments with her. He'd told her things he'd never told anyone else, like how his father, Frances's grandfather John, had let Hardwick pick out the color of the drapes and the rug. How John had let Hardwick try a new beer fresh off the line, and then made him tell the older man why it was good and what the brewers should do better.

"This office," her daddy used to say, "made me who I am." And then he'd give her a brief, rare hug and say, "And it'll make you who you are, too, my girl."

Ridiculous how the thought of a simple hug from her father could make her all misty-eyed.

She couldn't bear the thought of all this history—all *her* memories—being sold off to the highest bidder. Even if that would result in a tidy commission for her.

If she couldn't stop the sale, the best she could do was convince Chadwick to buy as much of his old office as possible. Her brother had fought to keep this company in the family. He'd understand that some things just couldn't be sold away.

But that wasn't plan A.

She tucked her tenderness away. In matters such as this one, tenderness was a liability, and God knew she couldn't afford any more of those.

So she stopped in the middle of the office and waited for Logan to catch up. She did not fold herself gracefully into one of the guest chairs in front of the desk, nor did she arrange herself seductively on the available love seat. She didn't even think of sprawling herself out on the conference table.

She stood in the middle of the room as though she was ruler of all she saw. And no one—not even a temporary CEO built like a linebacker—could convince her otherwise.

She was surprised when he did not slam the door shut. Instead, she heard the gentle whisper of it clicking closed. *Head up, shoulders back*, she reminded herself as she stood, waiting for him to make the next move. She would show him no mercy. She expected nothing but the same returned in kind.

She saw him move toward the conference table, where he draped her cape over the nearest chair. She felt his eyes on her. No doubt he was admiring her body even as he debated wringing her neck.

Men were so easy to confuse.

He was the kind of man, she decided, who would need to reassert his control over the situation. Now that the audience had dispersed, he would feel it a moral imperative to put her back in her place.

She could not let him get comfortable. It was just that simple.

Ah, she'd guessed right. He made a wide circle around her, not bothering to hide how he was checking out her best dress as he headed for the desk. Frances held her pose until he was almost seated. Then she reached into her small handbag—emerald-green silk, made to match the dress, of course—and pulled out a small mirror and lipstick. Ignoring Logan entirely, she fixed her lips, making sure to exaggerate her pouts.

Was she hearing things or had a nearly imperceptible groan come from the area behind the desk?

This was almost too easy, really.

She put the lipstick and mirror away and pulled out her phone. Logan opened his mouth to say something, but she interrupted him by taking a picture of the desk. And of him.

He snapped his mouth shut. "Frances *Beaumont*, huh?"

"The one and only," she purred, taking a close-up of the carved details on the corner of the desk. And if she had to bend over to do so—well, she couldn't help it if this dress was exceptionally low-cut.

"I suppose," Logan said in a strangled-sounding voice, "that there's no such thing as a coincidence?"

"I certainly don't believe in them." She shifted her angle and took another shot. "Do you?"

"Not anymore." Instead of sounding flummoxed or even angry, she detected a hint of humor in his voice. "I suppose you know your way around, then?"

"I do," she cheerfully agreed. Then she paused, as if she'd just remembered that she'd forgotten her manners. "I'm so sorry—I don't believe I caught your name?"

My, *that* was a look. But if he thought he could intimidate her, he had no idea who he was dealing with. "My apologies." He stood and held out his hand. "I'm Ethan Logan. I'm the CEO of the Beaumont Brewery."

She let his hand hang for a beat before she wrapped her fingers around his. He had hands that matched his shoulders—thick and strong. This Ethan Logan certainly didn't look a thing like the bean-counting lackey she'd pictured.

"Ethan," she said, dropping her gaze and looking up at him through her lashes.

His hand was warm as his fingers curled around her smaller hand. Strong, oh yes—he could easily break her hand. But he didn't. All the raw power he projected was clearly—and safely—locked down.

Instead, he turned her hand over and kissed the back of it. The very thing she'd implied he should do earlier, when they'd had an audience. It'd seemed like a safe move then, an action she knew he'd never take her up on.

But here? In the enclosed space of the office, with no one to witness his chivalrous gesture? She couldn't tell if the kiss was a threat or a seduction. Or both.

Then he raised his gaze and looked her in the eyes. Suddenly, the room was much warmer, the air much thinner. Frances had to use every ounce of her self-control not to take huge gulping breaths just to get some oxygen into her body. Oh, but he had nice eyes, warm and determined and completely focused on her.

She might have underestimated him.

Not that he needed to know that. She allowed herself an

innocent blush, which took some work. She hadn't been innocent for a long time. "A pleasure," she murmured, wondering how long he planned to kiss her hand.

"It's all mine," he assured her, straightening up and taking a step back. She noted with interest that he didn't sit back down. "So you're the appraiser Delores hired?"

"I hope you won't be too hard on her," she simpered, taking this moment to put another few steps between his body and hers.

"And why shouldn't I be? Are you even qualified to do this? Or did she just bring you in to needle me?"

He said it in far too casual a tone. *Damn.* His equilibrium was almost restored. She couldn't have that.

And what's more, she couldn't let him impinge on her ability to do this job.

Then she realized that his lips—which had, to this point, only been compressed into a thin line of anger or dropped open in shock—were curving into a far-too-cocky grin. He'd scored a hit on her, and he knew it.

She quickly schooled her face into the appropriate demureness, using the excuse of taking more pictures to do so.

"I am, in fact, highly qualified to appraise the contents of this office. I have a bachelor's degree in art history and a master's of fine art. I was the manager at Galerie Solaria for several years. I have extensive connections with the local arts scene."

She stated her qualifications in a light, matter-of-fact tone designed to put him at ease. Which, given the little donut stunt she'd pulled, would probably actually make him more nervous—if he had his wits about him. "And if anyone would know the true value of these objects," she added, straightening to give him her very best smile, "it'd be a Beaumont—don't you think? After all, this was ours for *so* long."

He didn't fall for the smile. Instead, he eyed her suspiciously, just as she'd suspected he would. She would have to reconsider her opinion of him. Now that the shock of her appearance was wearing off, he seemed more and more up to the task of playing this game.

Even though it shouldn't, the thought thrilled her. Ethan Logan would be a formidable opponent. This might even be fun. She could play the game with Ethan—a game she would win, without a doubt—and in the process, she could protect her family legacy and help out Delores and all the rest of the employees.

"How about you?" she asked in an offhand manner.

"What about me?" he asked.

"Are you qualified to run a company? This company?" She couldn't help it. The words came out a little sharper than she had wanted them to. But she followed up the questions with a fluttering of her eyelashes and another demure smile.

Not that they worked. "I am, in fact," he said in a mocking tone as he parroted her words, "highly qualified to run this company. I am a co-owner of my firm, Corporate Restructuring Services. I have restructured thirteen previous companies, raising stock prices and increasing productivity and efficiency. I have a bachelor's degree in economics and a master's of business administration, and I *will* turn this company around."

He said the last part with all the conviction of a man who truly believed himself to be on the right side of history.

"I'm quite sure you will." Of course she agreed with him. He was expecting her to argue. "Why, once the employees all get over that nasty flu that's been going around…" She lifted a shoulder, as if to say it was only a matter of time. "You'll have things completely under control within days." Then, just to pour a little lemon juice in the wound, she leaned forward. His gaze held—he didn't even glance at her cleavage. *Damn. Time to up the ante.*

She let her eyes drift over those massive shoulders and the broad chest. He was quite unlike the thin, pale men who populated the art world circles she moved within. She could still feel his lips on the back of her hand.

Oh, yes, she could play this game. For a short while, she could feel like Frances Beaumont again—powerful, beautiful, holding sway over everyone in her orbit. She could use Ethan Logan to get back what she'd lost in the past six months and—if she was very lucky—she might even be able to inflict some damage on AllBev through the Brewery. Corporate espionage and all that.

So she added in a confidential voice, "I have faith in your abilities."

"Do you?"

She looked him up and down again and smiled. A real smile this time, not one couched to elicit a specific response. "Oh, yes," she said, turning away from him. "I do."

Three

He needed her.

That crystal clear revelation was quickly followed by a second—and far more depressing one—Frances Beaumont would destroy him if he gave her half the chance.

As he watched Frances move around his office, taking pictures of the furniture and antiques and making completely harmless small talk about potential buyers, he knew he would have to risk the latter to get the former.

The way all those workers had been eating out of her hand—well, out of her donut box? The way not a single damn one of them had gotten back to work when he'd ordered them to—but they'd all jumped when Frances Beaumont had smiled at them?

It hurt to admit—even to himself—that the workers here would not listen to him.

But they would listen to her.

She was one of them—a Beaumont. They obviously adored her—even Delores, the old battle-ax, had bowed and scraped to this stunningly beautiful woman.

"If you wouldn't mind," she said in that delicate voice that he was completely convinced was a front. She kicked out of her shoes and lined one of the conference chairs up beneath a window. She held out her hand for him. "I'd like to get a better shot of the friezes over the windows."

"Of course," he said in his most diplomatic voice.

This woman—this stunning woman who's fingertips were light and warm against his hand as he helped her balance onto the chair, leaving her ass directly at eye level—had already ripped him to shreds several times over.

She was gorgeous. She was clearly intelligent. And she was obviously out to undermine him. That's what the donuts had been about. Announcing to the world in general and him in particular that this was still the Beaumont Brewery in every sense of the word.

"Thank you," she murmured, placing her hand on his shoulder to balance herself as she stepped down.

She didn't stick the landing, although he couldn't say if that was accidental or on purpose.

Before he could stop himself, his arm went around her waist to steady her.

Which was a mistake because electricity arced between them. She looked up at him through those lashes—he'd lost count of how many times she'd done that so far—but this time it hit him differently.

After almost a month of dealing with passive-aggressive employees terrified of being downsized he suddenly felt like a very different man altogether.

"Thank you," she said again, in a quiet whisper that somehow felt more honest, less calculated than almost every other word she'd uttered so far. Imperceptibly, she leaned into him. He could feel the heat of her breasts through his suit.

As soon as he was sure she wouldn't fall over, he stepped well clear of her. He needed her—but he could not need her like that. Not now, not ever. Because she *would* destroy him. He had no doubt about that. None.

Still…an idea was taking shape in his mind.

Maybe he'd been going about this all wrong. Instead of trying to strip the Beaumont out of the Beaumont Brew-

ery, maybe what he needed to do was bring in a Beaumont.
The moment the idea occurred to him, he latched on to it
with both hands.

Yes. What he really needed was to have a Beaumont on
board with the management changes he was implementing.
If the workers realized their old bosses were signing off
on the reorganization, there wouldn't be any more mass
food poisonings or flu or whatever they'd planned for next
week. Sure, there'd still be grumbling and personnel turn-
over, but if he had a Beaumont by his side...

"So!" Frances said brightly, just as she leaned over to
adjust the strap on her shoe.

Ethan had to slam his eyes shut so he wouldn't be caught
staring at her barely contained cleavage. If he was going
to pull this off, he had to keep his wits about him and his
pants zipped.

"How would you like to proceed? Ethan?" It was only
when she said his name that he figured it was safe to look.

As safe as it got, anyway. More than any other woman
he'd seen in person, Frances looked as if she'd walked right
off a movie screen and into his office. Her hair fell in soft
waves over her shoulders and her eyes were a light blue
that took on a greenish tone that matched her dress. She
was the stuff of fantasies, all luscious curves and soft skin.

"I want to hire you."

Direct was better. If he tried to dance around the subject, she'd spin him in circles.

It worked, too—at least for a second. Her eyes widened
in surprise, but she quickly got herself back under control.
She laughed lightly, like a chime tinkling in the wind. "Mr.
Logan," she said, beaming a high-wattage smile at him.
"You already have hired me. The furniture?" she reminded
him, looking around the room. "My family's legacy?"

"That's not what I mean," he replied. "I want you to
come work for me. Here. At the Brewery. As..." His mind

spun for something that would be appropriate to a woman like her. "As executive vice president of human resources. In charge of employee relations." *There*. That sounded fancy without actually meaning anything.

A hint of confusion wrinkled her forehead. "You want me to be a…manager?" She said the word as if it left a bad taste in her mouth. "Out of the question." But she favored him with that smile he'd decided she wielded like other people might wield a knife in a street fight. "I'm so sorry, but I couldn't possibly work for the Beaumont Brewery if it wasn't owned by an actual Beaumont." With crisp efficiency, she snatched up her cape and elegantly swirled it around her shoulders, hiding her body from his eyes.

Not that he was looking at it. He felt the corners of his mouth curve up in a smile. He had her off balance for possibly the first time since she'd walked onto the Brewery property.

"I'll work up an appraisal sheet and a list of potential buyers for some of the more sentimental pieces," she announced, not even bothering to look over her shoulder as she strode toward the door.

Before he realized what he was doing, he ran after her. "Wait," he said, getting to the door just as she put her hand on the knob. He pushed the door shut.

And then realized he basically had her trapped between the door and his body.

She knew it, too. Moving with that dancer's grace, she pivoted and leaned back, her breasts thrust toward him and her smile coy. "Did you need something else?"

"Won't you at least consider it?"

"About the job offer?" She grinned. It was too victorious to be pretty. "I rather think not."

What else would she be thinking about? His blood began to pound in his veins. He couldn't admit defeat, couldn't admit that a beautiful woman had spun him around until he hadn't realized he'd lost until it was too late. He had to come up with something to at least make her keep her options open. He could not run this company without her.

"Have dinner with me, then."

If this request surprised her, it didn't show. Instead, she tilted her head to one side, sending waves of beautiful red hair cascading over her cloaked shoulders. Then she moved. A hand emerged from the folds of her cloak and she touched him. She touched the line of his jaw with the tips of her fingers and then slid them down to where his white shirt was visible beneath the V of his suit jacket.

Heat poured off her as she flattened her palm against him. He desperately wanted to close his eyes and focus on the way her touch made his body jump to full attention. He wanted to lower his head and taste her ruby-red lips. He wanted to pull her body into his and feel her skin against his.

He did none of those things.

Instead, he took it like a man. Or he tried to. But when she said, in that soft whisper of hers, "And why would I agree to *that*?" it nearly broke his resolve.

"I'd like the chance to change your mind. About the job offer." Which was not strictly true, not any longer. Not when her palm moved in the smallest of circles over his heart.

"Is that all?" she breathed. He could feel the heat from her hand burning his skin. "There's nothing else you want from me?"

"I just want what's best for the company." Damn it all; his voice had gotten deeper on him. But he couldn't help it, not with the way she was looking up at him. "Don't you?"

Something in her face changed. It wasn't resignation, not really—and it wasn't surrender.

It was engagement. It was a *yes*.

She lightly pushed on his chest. He straightened and

dropped his arm away from the door. "Dinner. For the company," she agreed. He couldn't interpret that statement, not when his ears were ringing with desire. "Where are you staying?"

"I have a suite at the Hotel Monaco."

"Shall we say seven o'clock tomorrow night? In the lobby?"

"It would be an honor."

She arched an eyebrow at him, and then, with a swirling turn, she was gone, striding into the reception area and pausing only to thank Delores again for all her help.

He had to find a way to get Frances on his side.

It had nothing to do with the way he could still feel her touch burned into his skin.

Four

In the end, it'd come down to one of two dresses. Frances only had four left after the liquidation of her closet anyway. The green one was clearly out—it would reek of desperation to wear the same dress twice, even if Ethan's eyes had bugged out of his head when he'd looked at her in it.

She also had her bridesmaid's dress from her brother Phillip's wedding, a sleek gray one with rhinestone accents. But that felt too formal for dinner, even if it did look good on her.

Which meant she had to choose between the red velvet and the little black dress for her negotiation masquerading as dinner with Ethan Logan.

The red dress would render him completely speechless; that she knew. She'd always had a fondness for it—it transformed her into a proper lady instead of what she often felt like, the black sheep of the family.

But there was nothing subtle about the red dress. And besides, if the evening went well, she might need a higher-powered dress for later.

The little black dress was really the only choice. It was a halter-top style and completely backless. The skirt twirled out, but there was no missing the cleavage. The dark color made it appear more subdued at first, which would work to her advantage. If she paired it with her cropped bolero jacket, she could project an air of seriousness, and then, when she needed to befuddle Ethan, she could slip off the jacket. *Perfect.*

She made it downtown almost twenty minutes late, which meant she was right on schedule. Ethan Logan could sit and cool his heels for a bit. The more she kept him off balance, the better her position would be.

Which did beg the question—what was her position? She'd only agreed to dinner because he'd said he wanted what was best for the company. And the way he'd said it...

Well, she also wanted what was best for the company. But for her, that word was a big umbrella, under which the employees were just as important as the bottom line.

And after all, if something continued to be named the Beaumont Brewery, shouldn't it still be connected to the Beaumonts?

So dinner was strictly about those two objectives. She would see what she could get Ethan to reveal about the long-term plan for the Brewery. And if there was something in those plans that could help her get her world back in order, so much the better.

Yes, that was it. Dinner had nothing to do with how she'd felt Ethan's chest muscles twitch under her touch, nothing to do with the simmering heat that had rolled off him. And it had even less to do with the way he'd looked down at her, like a man who'd been adrift at sea for too long and had finally spotted land.

She was Frances Beaumont. She could not be landed. For years, she'd had men look at her as if they were starving and she was a banquet. It was nothing new. Just a testament to her name and genetics. Ethan Logan would be no different. She would take what she needed from him—that feeling that she was still someone who mattered, someone who wielded power—and leave the rest.

Which did not explain why, for the first time in what felt

like years, Frances had butterflies in her stomach as she strode into the lobby of the Hotel Monaco. Was she nervous? It wasn't possible. She didn't get nervous, especially not about something like this. She'd spent her entire life navigating the shark-infested waters of wealthy and powerful men. Ethan was just another shark. And he wasn't even a great white. He was barely a dogfish.

"Good evening, Ms. Beaumont."

"Harold," she said to the doorman with a warm smile and a big tip.

"Ms. Beaumont! How wonderful to see you again!" At this rather loud pronouncement, several other guests in the immediate vicinity paused to gape at her.

Frances ignored the masses. "Thank you, Heidi," she said to the clerk at the front desk with another warm smile. The hotel had been catering to the Beaumont family for years, and Frances liked to keep the staff on her side.

"And what can we do for you tonight?" Heidi asked.

"I'm meeting someone for dinner." She scanned the crowd, but she didn't see Ethan. He wouldn't be easy to miss—a man as massively built as he was? All those muscles would stand out.

Then she saw him. And did a double take. Yes, those shoulders, that neck, were everything she remembered them being. The clothing, however? Unlike the conservative gray suit and dull tie he'd had on in the office, he was wearing a pair of artfully distressed jeans, a white button-up shirt without a tie and…a purple sports coat? A deep purple—plum, maybe. She would not have figured he was the kind of man who would stand outside a sartorial box with any great flair—or success.

When he saw her, he pushed himself off the column he was leaning against. "Frances, hello." Which was a perfectly normal thing to say. But he said it as if he couldn't quite believe his eyes—or his luck—as she strode to-ward him.

He should feel lucky. "Ethan." When he held out his hand, she took it and used it to pull herself up so she could kiss him on the cheek.

His free hand rested against her side, steadying her. "You look amazing," he murmured, his mouth close to her ear.

Warmth that bordered on heat started where his breath kissed her skin and flamed out over her body. That was what made her nervous. Not the man, not the muscula-ture—not even his position as CEO of her family's com-pany.

It was the way her body reacted to him. The way a touch, a look—a whispered word—could set her fluttering. *Ridiculous*. She was not flattered by his attentions. This was not a date. This was corporate espionage in a great dress. This was her using what few resources she had left at her disposal to get her life back on track. This was about her disarming Ethan Logan, not the other way around.

So she clamped down on the shiver that threatened to race across her skin as she lowered herself away from him. "That's a great color on you. Very…" She let the word hang in the air for a beat too long. "Bold," she finished. "Not just any man could pull off that look."

He raised his eyebrows. She realized he was trying not to laugh at her. "Says the woman who showed up in an emerald evening gown to hand out donuts. Have no fear, I'm comfortable in my masculinity. Shall we? I made res-ervations at the restaurant." He held out his arm for her.

"We shall." She lightly placed her hand in the crook of his elbow. She didn't need his help—she could walk in these shoes just fine—but this was part of setting him up. It had nothing to do with wanting another flash of heat from where their bodies met.

The restaurant was busy, as was to be expected on a Saturday night. When they entered, the diners paused. She and Ethan must have made quite a pair, her with her red hair and him in his purple jacket.

People were already forming opinions. That was something she could use to her advantage. She placed her free hand on top of Ethan's arm and leaned into him. Not much, but just enough to create the impression that this was a date.

The maître d' led them to a small table tucked in a dim corner. They ordered—she got the lobster, just to be obnoxious about it, and he got the steak, just to be predictable—and Ethan ordered a bottle of pinot grigio.

Then they were alone. "I'm glad you came out tonight."

She demurely placed her hands in her lap. "Did you think I would cancel?"

"I wouldn't have been surprised if you'd tried to string me along a little bit. Just to watch me twist." He said it in a jovial way but she didn't miss the edge to his voice.

So he wasn't totally befuddled. And he was more than sharp enough to know they were here for something much more than dinner.

That didn't mean she had to own up to it. "Whatever do you mean?"

His smile sharpened. The silence carried, and she was in serious danger of fidgeting nervously under his direct gaze.

She was saved by the sommelier, who arrived with the wine. Frances desperately wanted to take a long drink, but she could not let Ethan know he was unsettling her. So she slowly twirled the stem of her wineglass until he said, "I propose a toast."

"Do you now?"

"To a long and productive partnership." She did not drink. Instead, she leveled a cool gaze at him over the rim of her glass and waited for him to notice. Which, admittedly, did not take long. "Yes?"

"I'm not taking that job, you know. I have 'considered' it, and I can't imagine a more boring job in the history of employment," she told him.

She would not let the world know she was so desperate as to take a job in management at a company that used to belong to her family. She might be down on her luck, but she wasn't going to give up.

Then, and only then, did she allow herself to sip her wine. She had to be careful. She needed to keep her wits about her and not let the wine—and all those muscles—go to her head.

"I figured as much," he said with a low chuckle that Frances felt right in her chest. What was it with this man's voice?

"Then why would you toast to such a thing?" Maybe now was the time to take the jacket off? He seemed entirely too self-aware. She did not have the advantage here, not like she'd had in the office.

Oh, she did not like that smile on him. Well, she did—she might actually like it a great deal, if she wasn't the one in the crosshairs.

He leaned forward, his gaze so intense that she considered removing her jacket just to cool down. "I'm sure you know why I want you," he all but growled.

It *was* getting hotter in here. She tried to look innocent. It was the only look she could pull off with the level of blush she'd probably achieved by now. "My sparkling wit?"

There was a brief crack in his serious facade, as if her sparkling wit was the correct answer. "I consider that a fringe benefit," he admitted with a tilt of his head. "But let's not play dumb, you and I. It's far too beneath a woman with your considerable talents. And your talents..." She straightened her back and thrust her chest out in a desperate attempt to throw him off balance. It didn't work. His gaze never left her face. "Your talents are considerable. I'm not sure I've ever met a woman like you before."

"Are you hitting on me?"

The corner of his mouth quirked up, making him look like a predator. She might have to revise her earlier opinion of him. He was *not* a dogfish. More like…a tiger shark, sleek and fast. Able to take her down before she even realized she was in danger.

"Of course not."

"Then why do you want me?" Because honestly—for the first time in her adult life—she wasn't sure what the answer would be.

Men wanted her. They always had. The moment her boobs had put in an appearance, she'd learned about base male lust—how to provoke it, how to manage it, how to use it for her own ends. Men wanted her for a simple, carnal reason. And after watching stepmother after stepmother come and go out of her father's life, she had resolved never to be used. Not like that.

The upside was that she'd never had her heart broken. But the downside?

She'd never been in love. Self-preservation, however vital to survival, was a lonely way to live.

"It's simple, really." He leaned back, his posture at complete ease. "Obviously, everyone at the Brewery hates me. I can't blame them—no one likes change, especially when they have to change against their will." He grinned at her, a sly thing. "I should probably be surprised that Delores hasn't spiked my coffee with arsenic by now."

"Probably," she agreed. Where was he going with this?

"But you?" He reached over and picked up her hand, rubbing his thumb along the edges of her fingertips. Against her will, she shivered—and he felt it. That smile deepened—his voice deepened. Everything deepened. *Oh, hell.*

"I saw how the workers—especially the lifers—responded to you and your donut stunt," he went on, still stroking her hand. "There's nothing they wouldn't do for you, and probably wouldn't do for any Beaumont."

"If you think this is going to convince me to take that job, you're sorely mistaken," she replied. She wanted to jerk her hand out of his—she needed to break that skin-to-skin contact—but she didn't. If this was how the game was going to go, then she needed to be all in.

So instead she curled her fingers around his and made small circles on the base of his palm with her thumb. She was justly rewarded with a little shiver from him. *Okay, good. Great.* She wasn't entirely at his mercy here. She could still have an impact even without the element of surprise. "Especially if you're going to call them 'lifers.' That's insulting. You make them sound like prisoners."

He notched an eyebrow at her. "What would you call them?"

"Family." The simple reply—which was also the truth—was out before she could stop it.

She didn't know what she expected him to do with that announcement, but lifting her hand to his lips and pressing a kiss against her skin wasn't it. "And that," he whispered against her skin, "is exactly why I need you."

This time, she did pull her hand away. She dropped it into her lap and fixed him with her best polite glare, the one that could send valets and servers scurrying for cover. Just then, the waiter appeared with their food—and did, in fact, pause when Frances turned that glare in his direction. He set their plates down with a minimum of fanfare and all but sprinted away.

She didn't touch her food. "I'm hearing an awful lot about how much you need me. So let us, as you said, dispense with the games. I do not now, nor have I ever, formally worked for the Beaumont Brewery. I do not now, nor have I ever, had sex with a man who thought he was entitled to a piece of the Beaumont Brewery and, by extension, a piece of me. I will not take a desk job to help you win the approval of people you clearly dislike."

"They disliked me first," he put in as he cut his steak.

What she really wanted to do was throw her wine in his face. It'd feel so good to let loose and let him have it. Despite his claims that he recognized her intelligence, she had the distinct feeling that he was playing her, and she did not like it. "Regardless. What do you want, Mr. Logan? Because I'm reasonably certain that it's no longer just the dismantling and sale of my family's history."

He set his knife and fork aside and leaned his elbows on the table. "I need you to help me convince the workers that joining the current century is the only way the company will survive. I need you to help me show them that it doesn't have to be me against them or them against me— that we can work together to make the Brewery something more than it was."

She snorted. "I'll be sure to pass such touching sentiments along to my brother—the man you replaced."

"By all accounts, he was quite the businessman. I'm sure that he'd agree with me. After all, he made significant changes to the management structure himself after his father passed. But he was constrained by that sense of family you so aptly described. I am not."

"All the good it's doing you." She took another sip of wine, a slightly larger one than before.

"You see my problem. If the workers fight me on this, it won't be only a few people who lose their jobs—the entire company will shut down, and we will all suffer."

She tilted her head from side to side, considering. "Perhaps it should. The Beaumont Brewery without a Beaumont isn't the same thing, no matter what the marketing department says."

"Would you really give your blessing to job losses for hundreds of workers, just for the sake of a name?"

"It's *my* name," she shot at him.

But he was right. If the company went down in flames, it'd burn the people she cared for. Her brothers would be safe—they'd already ensconced themselves in the Percheron Drafts brewery. But Bob and Delores and all the rest? The ones who'd whispered to her how nervous they were about the way the wind was blowing? Who were afraid for their families? The ones who knew they were too old to start over, who were scared that they'd be forced into early retirement without the generous pension benefits the Beaumont Brewery had always offered its loyal employees?

"Which brings us back to the heart of the matter. I need you."

"No, you don't. You need my approval." Her lobster was no doubt getting cold, but she didn't have much of an appetite at the moment.

Something that might have been a smile played over his lips. For some reason, she took it as a compliment, as if he was acknowledging her intelligence for real this time, instead of paying lip service to it. "Why didn't you go into the family business? You'd have made a hell of a negotiator."

"I find business, in general, to be beneath me." She cast a cutting look at him. "Much like many of the people who willingly choose to engage in it."

He laughed then, a real thing that she wished grated on her ears and her nerves but didn't. It was a warm sound, full of humor and honesty. It made her want to smile. She didn't. "I'm not going to take the job."

"I wasn't going to offer it to you again. You're right—it is beneath you."

Here it came—the trap he was waiting to spring. He leaned forward, his gaze intent on hers and in the space of a second, before he spoke, she realized what he was about to say. All she could think was, *Oh, hell*.

"I don't want to hire you. I want to marry you."

Five

The weight of his statement hit Frances so hard Ethan was surprised she didn't crumple in the chair.

But of course she didn't. She was too refined, too schooled to let her shock show. Even so, her eyes widened and her mouth formed a perfect O, kissable in every regard.

"You want to...what?" Her voice cracked on the last word.

Turnabout is fair play, he decided as he let her comment hang in the air. She'd caught him completely off guard in the office yesterday and had clearly thought she could keep that shock and awe going. But tonight? The advantage was his.

"I want to marry you. More specifically, I want you to marry me," he explained. Saying the words out loud made his blood hum. When he'd come up with this plan, it had seemed like a bold-yet-risky business decision. He'd quickly realized that Frances Beaumont would absolutely not take a desk job, but the unavoidable fact was he needed her approval to validate his restructuring plans.

And what better way to show that the Beaumonts were on board with the restructuring than if he were legally wed to the favored daughter?

Yes, it had all seemed cut-and-dried when he'd formulated the plan last night. A sham marriage, designed to

bolster his position within the company. He'd done a little digging into her past and discovered that she had tried
to launch some sort of digital art gallery recently, but it'd
gone under. So she might need funding. No problem.

But he'd failed to take into account the actual woman
he'd just proposed to. The fire in her eyes more than
matched the fire in her hair, and all of her lit a hell of a
flame in him. He had to shift in his chair to avoid discom-
fort as he tried not to look at her lips.

"You want to get married?" She'd recovered some, the
haughty tone of her voice overcoming her surprise. "How
very flattering."

He shrugged. He'd planned for this reaction. Frankly,
he'd expected nothing less, not from her.

He hadn't planned for the way her hand—her skin—had
felt against his. But a plan was a plan, and he was in for far
more than a penny. "Of course, I'm not about to profess
my undying love for you. Admiration, yes." Her cheeks
colored slightly. Nope, he hadn't planned for that, either.

Suddenly, his bold plan felt like the height of foolish-
ness.

"My," she murmured. Her voice was soft, but he didn't
miss the way it sliced through the air. "How I love to hear
sweet nothings. They warm a girl's heart."

He grinned again. "I'm merely proposing an…arrange-
ment, if you will. Open to negotiation. I already know a job
in management is not for you." He sat back, trying to look
casual. "I'm a man of considerable influence and power.
Is there something you need that I can help you with?"

"Are you trying to *buy* me?" Her fingertips curled
around the stem of her wineglass. He kept one hand on
the napkin in his lap, just in case he found himself wearing the wine.

"As I said, this isn't a proposal based on love. It's based
on need. You're already fully aware of how much I need

you. I'm just trying to ascertain what you need to make this arrangement worth your time. Above and beyond making sure that your Brewery family is well taken care of, that is." He leaned forward again. He enjoyed negotiations like this—probing and prodding to find the other party's breaking point. And a little bit of guilt never hurt anything.

"What if I don't want to marry you? Surely you can't think you're the first man who's ever proposed to me out of the blue." The dismissal was slight, but it carried weight. She was doing her level best to toy with him.

And he'd be lying if he said he didn't enjoy it. "I have no doubt you've been fending off men for years. But this proposal isn't based on want." However, that didn't stop his gaze from briefly drifting down to her chest. She had *such* an amazing body.

Her lips tightened, and she fiddled with the button on her jacket. "Then what's it based on?"

"I'm proposing a short-term arrangement. A marriage of convenience. Love doesn't need to play a role."

"Love?" she asked, batting her eyelashes. "There's more to a marriage than that."

"Point. Lust also is not a part of my proposal. A one-year marriage. We don't have to live together. We don't have to sleep together. We need to occasionally be seen in public together. That's it."

She blinked at him. "You're serious, aren't you? What kind of marriage would *that* be?"

Now it was Ethan's turn to fidget with his wineglass. He didn't want to get into the particulars of his parents' marriage at the moment. "Suffice it to say, I've seen long-distance marriages work out quite well for all parties involved."

"How delightful," she responded, disbelief dripping off every word. "Are you gay?"

"What? No!" He jolted so hard that he almost knocked

his glass over. "I mean, not that there's anything wrong with that. But I'm not."

"Pity. I might consider a loveless, sexless marriage to a gay man. Sadly," she went on in a not-sad voice, "I don't trust you to hold up your sexless end of the bargain."

"I'm not saying we couldn't have sex." In fact, given the way she'd pressed her lips to his cheek earlier, the way she'd held his hand—he'd be perfectly fine with sex with her. "I'm merely saying it's not expected. It's not a deal breaker."

She regarded him with open curiosity. "So let me see if I understand this proposal, such as it is. You'd like me to marry you and lend the weight of the Beaumont name to your destruction of the Beaumont Brewery—"

"Reconstruction, not destruction," he interrupted.

She ignored him. "In a starter marriage that has a built-in sunset at one year, no other strings attached?"

"That sums it up."

"Give me one good reason why I shouldn't stab you in the hand with my knife."

He flinched. "Actually, I was waiting for you to give me a good reason." She looked at him flatly. "I read online that your digital art gallery recently failed." He said it gently. He could sympathize with a well-thought-out project going sideways—or backward.

She rested her hand on her knife. But she didn't say anything. Her eyes—beautiful light eyes that walked the line between blue and green—bore into him.

"If there was something that I—as an investor—could help you with," he went on, keeping his voice quiet, "well, that could be part of our negotiation. It'd be venture capital—*not* an attempt to buy you," he added. She took her hand off her knife and put it in her lap, which Ethan took as a sign that he'd hit the correct nerve. He went on, "I wouldn't—and couldn't—cut you a personal check. But as an angel investor, I'm sure we could come to terms you'd find satisfactory."

"Interesting use of the word *angel* there," she said. Her voice was quiet. None of the seduction or coquettishness that she'd wielded like a weapon remained.

Finally, he was talking to the real Frances Beaumont. No more artifice, no more layers. Just a beautiful, intelligent woman. A woman he'd just proposed to.

This was for the job, he reminded himself. He was only proposing because he needed to get control of the Beaumont Brewery, and Frances Beaumont was the shortest, straightest line between where he was today and where he needed to be. It had nothing to do with the actual woman.

"Do you do this often? Propose marriage to women connected with the businesses you're stripping?"

"No, actually. This would be a first for me."

She picked up her knife, and he unwittingly tensed. One corner of her perfect rosebud mouth quirked into a smile before she began to cut into her lobster tail. "Really? I suppose I should be flattered."

He began to eat his steak. It had cooled past the optimal temperature, but he figured that was the price one paid for negotiating before the main course arrived. "I'm never in one city for more than a year, usually only for a few months. I have, on occasion, made the acquaintance of a woman with whom I enjoy doing things such as this—dining out, seeing the sights."

"Having sex?" she asked bluntly.

She was trying to unnerve him again. It might be working. "Yes, when we're both so inclined. But those were short-term, no-commitment relationships, as agreed upon by both parties."

"Just a way to pass the time?"

"That might sound harsh, but yes. If you agree to the

arrangement, we could dine out like this, maybe attend the theater or whatever it is you do for fun here in Denver."

"This isn't exactly a one-horse town anymore, you know. We have theaters and gala benefits and art openings and a football team. Maybe you've heard of them?" Her gaze drifted down to his shoulders. "You might consider trying out for the front four."

Ethan straightened his shoulders. He wasn't a particularly vain man, but he kept himself in shape, and he'd be lying if he said he wasn't flattered that she'd noticed. "I'll keep it in mind."

They ate in silence. He decided it was her play. She hadn't stabbed him, and she hadn't thrown a drink in his face. He put the odds of getting her to go along with this plan at fifty-fifty.

And if she didn't... Well, he'd need a new plan.

Her lobster tail was maybe half-eaten when she set her cutlery aside. "I've never fielded a marriage proposal like yours before."

"How many have you fielded?"

She waved the question away. "I've lost count. A quickie wedding, a one-year marriage with no sex, an irreconcilable-differences, uncontested divorce—all in exchange for an investment into a property or project of my choice?"

"Basically." He'd never proposed before. He couldn't tell if her no-nonsense tone was a good sign or not. "We'd need a prenup."

"Obviously." She took a much longer pull on her wine. "I want five million."

"I'm sorry?"

"I have a friend who wants to launch a new art gallery, with me as the co-owner. She has a business plan worked up and a space selected. All we need is the capital." She pointed a long, red-tipped nail at him. "And you did offer to invest, did you not?"

She had him there. "I did. Do we have a deal?" He stuck out his hand and waited.

She must be out of her ever-loving mind.

As Frances regarded the hand Ethan had extended toward her, she was sure she had crossed some line from desperation into insanity to even consider his offer.

Would she really agree to marry the living embodiment of her family's downfall for what, essentially, was the promise of job security after he was gone? With five million—a too-large number she'd pulled out of thin air—she and Becky could open that gallery in grand style, complete with all the exhibitions and parties it took to wine and dine wealthy art patrons.

This time, it'd be different. It was Becky's business plan, after all. Not Frances's. But even that thought stung a bit. Becky's plan had a chance of working. Unlike all of Frances's grand plans.

She needed this. She needed something to go her way, something to work out right for once. With a five-million-dollar investment, she and Becky could get the gallery operational and Frances could move out of the Beaumont mansion. Even if she only lived in the apartment over the gallery, it'd still be hers. She could go back to being Frances Beaumont. She could feel like a grown-up in control of her own life.

All it'd take would be giving up that control for a year. Not just giving it up, but giving it to Ethan.

She felt as if she was on the verge of passing out, but she refused to betray a single sign of panic. She did not breathe in deep gulps. She did not drop her head in her hands. And she absolutely did not fiddle with anything.

She kept herself serene and calm and did all her panicking on the inside, where no one could see it.

"Well?" Ethan asked. But it wasn't a gruff demand for an answer. His tone was more cautious than that.

And then there was the man himself. This was all quite noble, this talk of no sex and no emotions. But that didn't change the fact of the matter—Ethan Logan was one hell of a package. He could make her shiver and shake with the kind of heat she hadn't felt in a very long time.

Not that it mattered, because it didn't.

"I don't believe in love," she announced, mostly to see what kind of reaction it'd get.

"You don't? That seems unusually cynical for a woman of your age and beauty."

She didn't try to hide her eye roll. "I only mention it because if you're thinking about pulling one of those 'I'll make her love me over time' stunts, it's best to nip it in the bud right now."

She'd seen what people did in the name of love. How they made grand promises they had every intention of keeping until the next pretty face came along. As much as she'd loved her father, she hadn't been blind to his wandering eye or his wandering hands. She'd seen exactly what had happened to her mother, Jeannie—all because she'd believed in the power of love to tame the untamable Hardwick Beaumont.

"I wouldn't dream of it." Ethan's hand still hung in the air between them.

"I won't love you," she promised him, putting her palm in his. "I'd recommend you not love me."

Something in his eyes tightened as his fingers closed around hers. "I hope admiration is still on the table?"

She let her gaze drift over his body again. It wasn't desire, not really. She was an art connoisseur, and she was merely admiring his form. And wondering how it'd function. "I suppose."

"When do you want to get married?"

She thought it over. *Married.* The word felt weird rattling around her head. She'd never wanted to be married, never wanted to be tied to someone who could hurt her.

Of course, her brother Phillip had recently had a fairy-tale wedding that had been everything she might have ever wanted, if she'd actually wanted it. Which she didn't.

No, a big public spectacle was not the way to go here. This was, by all public appearances, a whirlwind romance, starting yesterday when she'd sashayed into his office. "I think we should cultivate the impression that we are swept up in the throes of passion."

"Agreed."

"Let's get married in two weeks."

Just saying it out loud made her want to hyperventilate. What would her brothers say to this, her latest stunt in a long line of stunts? "Frannie," she could practically hear Chadwick intone in his too-serious voice. "I don't think…" And Matthew? He was the one who always wanted everyone to line up and smile for the cameras and look like a big happy family. What would he say when she up and got herself hitched?

Then there was Byron, her twin. She'd thought she'd known Byron better than any other person in the world, and vice versa. But in the matter of a few weeks, he'd gone from her brother to a married man with a son and another baby on the way. Well, if anyone would understand her sudden change in matrimonial status, it'd be Byron.

Everyone else—especially Chadwick and Matthew—would just have to deal. This was her life. She could damn well do what she pleased with it.

Even if that meant marrying Ethan Logan.

Six

Ethan didn't know if it was the wine or the woman, but throughout the rest of dinner, he felt light-headed.

He was going to get married. To Frances Beaumont. In two weeks.

Which was great. Everything was going according to plan. He would demonstrate to the world that the Beaumonts were behind the restructuring of the Beaumont Brewery. That would buy him plenty of goodwill at the Brewery.

Yup. It was a great plan. There was just one major catch.

Frances leaned toward him and shrugged her jacket off. The sight of her bare shoulders hammered a spike of desire up his gut. He wasn't used to this sort of craving. Even when he found a lady friend to keep him company during his brief stints in cities around the country, he didn't usually succumb to this much *lust.*

His previous relationships were founded on...well, on *not* lust. Companionship was a part of it, sure. The sex was a bonus, definitely. And the women he consorted with were certainly lovely.

But the way he reacted to Frances? That was something else. Something different.

Something that threatened to break free from him.

Which was ridiculous. He was the boss. He was in control of this—all of this. The situation, his desires—

Well, maybe not his desires, not when Frances leaned forward and looked up at him coyly through her lashes. It shouldn't work, but it did.

"Well, then. Shall we get started?"

"Started?" But the word died on his lips when she reached across the table and ran her fingertips over his chin.

"Started," she agreed. She held out her hand, and he took it. He had no choice. "I happen to know a thing or two about creating a public sensation. We're already off to a great start, what with the confrontation outside your office and now this very public dinner. Kiss my hand again."

He did as he was told, pressing her skin against his lips and getting a hint of expensive perfume and the underlying taste of Frances.

He looked up to find her beaming at him, the megawatt smile probably visible from out on the sidewalk. But it wasn't real. Even he could tell that.

"So, kissing hands is on the table?" He didn't move her hand far from his mouth. He didn't want to.

When had he lost his head this much? When had he been this swamped by raw, unadulterated want? He needed to get his head back out of his pants and focus. He had explicitly promised that he would not make sex a deal breaker. He needed to keep his word, or the deal would be done before it got started.

"Oh, yes," she purred. Then she flipped her hand over in his grip and traced his lower lip with her thumb. "I'd imagine that there are several things still on the table."

Such as? His blood was beating a new, merciless rhythm in his veins, driving that spike of desire higher and higher until he was in actual pain. His mind helpfully supplied several vivid images that involved him, Frances and a table.

He caught her thumb in his mouth and sucked on it, his tongue tracing the edge of her perfectly manicured nail. Her eyes widened with desire, her pupils dilating until he could barely see any of the blue-green color at all. He swore he could see her nipples tighten through the fabric of her dress. Oh, yeah—a table, a bed—any flat surface would do. It didn't even have to be flat. Good sex could be had standing up.

He let go of her thumb and kissed her hand again. "Do you want to get out of here?"

"I'd like that," she whispered back.

It took a few minutes to settle the bill, during which every single look she shot him only made his blood pound that much harder. When had he been this overcome with lust? When had a simple business arrangement become an epic struggle?

She stood, and he realized the dress was completely backless. The wide swath of smooth, creamy skin that was Frances's back lay bare before him. His fingers itched to trace the muscles, to watch her body twitch under his touch.

He didn't want her to put her jacket back on and cover up that beautiful skin. And, thankfully, she didn't. She waited for him to assist her with her chair and then said, "Will you carry my jacket for me?"

"Of course." He folded it over one arm and then offered his other to her.

She leaned into his touch, her gorgeous red curls brushing against his shoulder. "Did you ever play football?" she asked, running her hands up and down his forearms. "Or were you just born this way?"

There was something he was supposed to be remembering, something that was important about Frances. But he couldn't think about anything but the way she'd looked in that green dress yesterday and the way she looked right now. The way he felt when she touched him.

He flexed under her hands and was rewarded with a little gasp from her. "I played. I got a scholarship to play in college, but I blew out my knee."

They were walking down the long hallway that separated the restaurant from the hotel. Then it'd be a quick turn to the left and into the elevators. A man could get into a lot of trouble in an elevator.

But they didn't even make it to the elevator. The moment they got to the middle of the lobby, Frances reached across his chest and slid her hand under his coat. Just like it had in the office yesterday, her touch burned him.

"Oh, that sounds awful," she breathed, curling her fingers around his shirt and pulling him toward her.

The noise of the lobby faded away until there was only the touch of her hand and the beating of his heart.

He turned into her, lowering his head. "Terrible," he agreed, but he no longer knew what they were talking about. All he knew was that he was going to kiss her.

Their lips met. The kiss was tentative at first as he tested her and she tested him. But then her mouth opened for him, and his control—the control he'd maintained for years and years, the control that made him a savvy businessman with millions in the bank—shattered on him.

He tangled his hands into her hair and roughly pulled her up to his mouth so he could taste her better—taste all of her. Dimly, somewhere in the back of his mind where at least three brain cells were doing their best to think about something beyond Frances's touch, Frances's taste—dimly, he realized they were standing in the middle of a crowd, although he'd forgotten exactly where they were.

There was a wolf whistle. And a second one—this one accompanied by laughter.

Frances pulled away, her impressive chest heaving and her eyes glazed with lust. "Your suite," she whispered, and then her tongue darted out, tracing a path on her lips that he needed to follow.

"Yeah. Sure." She could have suggested jumping out of an airplane at thirty thousand feet and he would have done it. Just so long as she went down with him.

Somehow, despite the tangle of arms and jackets, they made it to the elevators and then onto one. Other people were waiting, but no one joined them on the otherwise-empty lift. "Sorry," Frances said to the waiting guests as she curled up against his chest. "We'll send it back down," she added as the doors closed and shut them away from the rest of the world.

Then they were alone. Ethan slid his hands down her bare back before he cupped her bottom. "Where were we?"

"Here," she murmured, pressing her lips against his neck, right above his collar. "And here." Her teeth scraped over his skin as she pressed the full length of her body against his. "And…here."

She didn't touch him through his pants, not with her hands—but with her body? She shifted against him, and the pressure drove those last three rational brain cells out of his mind. "God, yes," he groaned, fisting his hands into her curls and tilting her head back. "How could I forget?"

He didn't give her time to reply. He crushed his mouth against hers. There wasn't any more time for testing kisses—all that existed in the safe space of this little moving room was his need for her and, given the way she was kissing him back, her need for him.

He liked sex—he always had. He prided himself on being good at it. But had he ever been this excited? This consumed with need? He couldn't remember. He couldn't think, not with Frances moaning into his mouth and arching her back, pushing her breasts into his body.

He reached up and started to undo the tie at the back of her neck, but she grabbed his hand and held it at waist height. "We're almost there," she murmured in a coy tone. "Can you wait just a little longer?"

No. "Yes."

Love and sex and, yes, marriage—that was all about waiting. There'd never been any instant gratification in it for him. He'd waited until he'd been eighteen before losing his virginity because it was a test of sorts. Everyone else was going as fast as they could, but Ethan was different. Better. He could resist the fire. He would not get burned.

Frances shifted against him again, and he groaned in the most delicious agony that had ever consumed him. Her touch—even through his clothing—seared him. For the first time in his life, he wanted to dance with the flames.

One flame—one flame-haired woman—in particular. Oh, how they would dance.

The elevator dinged. "Is this us?" Frances asked in a shaky whisper.

"This way." He grabbed her hand and strode out of the elevator. It was perhaps not the most gentlemanly way of going about it—essentially dragging her in her impossible shoes along behind him—but he couldn't help himself. If she couldn't walk, he'd carry her.

His suite was at the end of a long, quiet hall. The only noise that punctuated the silence was the sound of his blood pounding in his temples, pushing him faster until he was all but running, pulling Frances in his wake. Each step was pain and pleasure wrapped in one, his erection straining to do anything but walk. Or run.

After what felt like an hour of never-ending journeying, he reached his door. Torturous seconds passed as he tried to get the key card to work. Then the door swung open and he was pulling her inside, slamming the door shut behind them and pinning her against it. Her hands curled into his shirt, holding him close.

He must have had one lone remaining brain cell functioning, because instead of ripping that dress off her body so he could feast himself upon it, he paused to say, "Tell me what you want."

Because whatever she wanted was what he wanted.

Or maybe she wasn't holding him close. The thought occurred to him belatedly, just about the time her mouth curved up into what was a decidedly nonseductive smile. She pushed on his chest, and he had no choice but to let her. "Anything I want?"

She'd pushed him away, but her voice was still colored with craving, with a need he could feel more than hear. Maybe she wanted him to tie her up. Maybe she wanted to tie him up instead. Whatever it was, he was game.

"Yeah." He tried to lean back down to kiss her again, but she was strong for a woman her size. She held him back.

"I wonder what's on TV?"

It took every ounce of her willpower to push Ethan back, to push herself away from the door, but she did it anyway. She forced herself to stroll casually over to the dresser that held the flat-screen television and grab the remote. Then, without daring to look at Ethan, she flopped down on the bed. It was only after she'd propped herself up on her elbows and turned on the television that she hazarded a look at him.

He was leaning against the door. His jacket was half off; his shirt was a rumpled mess. He looked as though she'd mauled him. She was a little hazy on the details, but, as best she could recall, she had.

She turned her attention back to the television, randomly clicking without actually seeing what was onscreen. She'd only meant to put on a little show for the crowd. If they were going to do this sham marriage thing in two weeks, they needed to start their scandalous activities right now. Kissing in a lobby, getting into the elevator together? She was unmistakable with her red hair. And Ethan—he wasn't that hard to look up. People would make the connection. And people, being reliable, would talk.

When she'd stroked his face at dinner, she'd seen the headlines in her mind. "Whirlwind Romance between Beaumont Heir and New Brewery CEO?" That was what Ethan wanted, wasn't it? The air of Beaumont approval. This was nothing but a PR ploy.

Except...

Except for the way he'd kissed her. The way he'd kept kissing her.

At some point between when he'd sucked on her thumb and the kiss in the lobby—the first one, she mentally corrected—the game they'd been playing had changed.

It was all supposed to have been for show. But the way he had pinned her against the door in this very nice room? The way his deep voice had begged her to tell him what she wanted?

That hadn't felt like a game. That hadn't been for show.

The only thing that had kept her from spinning right over the edge was the knowledge that he didn't want her. Oh, he wanted her—naked, that was—but he didn't want *her*, Frances—complicated and crazy and more than a little lost. He'd only touched her because he wanted something, and she could not allow that to cloud her thinking.

"What—" He cleared his throat, but it didn't make his voice any stronger. "What are you doing?"

"Watching television." She kicked her heels up.

She cut another side glance at Ethan. He hadn't moved. "Why?"

It took everything Frances had to make herself sound glib and light. "What else are we going to do?"

His mouth dropped down to his chest. "I don't mean to sound crass, but…sex?"

Frances couldn't help it. Her gaze drifted down to the impressive bulge in his pants—the same bulge that had ground against her in the elevator.

Sex. The thought of undoing those pants and letting that bulge free sent an uncontrollable shiver down her back. She snapped her eyes back to the television screen. "Really," she said in a dismissive tone.

There was a moment where the only noise in the room was the sound of Ethan breathing heavily and some salesman on TV yelling about a cleaning cloth.

"Then what was that all about?" Ethan gruffly demanded.

"Creating an impression." She did not look at him.

"And who were we impressing in the elevator?"

She put on her most innocent look—which, granted, would have been a lot easier if her nipples weren't still chafing against the front of her dress. "Fine. A test, then."

Ethan was suddenly in front of the television, arms crossed as he glared down at her. "A *test*?"

"It has to be convincing, this relationship we're pretending to have," she explained, making a big show of looking around his body, rather than at the still-obvious bulge in his pants. "But part of the deal was that we don't have sex." She let that sink in before adding, "You're not going to back out of the deal, are you?"

Because that was a risk, and she knew it. There were many ways a deal could go south—especially when sex was on the line.

"You're testing *me*?" He took a step to the side, trying to block her view of the screen again.

"I won't marry just anyone, you know. I have standards."

She could feel the weight of his glare on her face, but

she refused to allow her skin to flush. She leaned the other way. Not that she had any idea of what she was watching. Her every sense was tuned into Ethan.

It'd be so easy to change her mind, to tell him that he'd passed his first test and that she had another test in mind—one that involved less clothing for everyone. She could find out what was behind that bulge and whether or not he knew how to use it.

She could have a few minutes where she wouldn't have to feel alone and adrift, where she could lose herself in Ethan. But that was all it would be. A few minutes.

And then the sex would be done, and she'd go back to being broke, unemployed Frances who was trading on her good looks even as they began to slip away. And Ethan? Well, he'd probably still marry her and fund her art gallery. But he'd know her in a way that felt too intimate, too personal.

Not that she was a shy, retiring virgin—she wasn't. But she had to keep her eye on the long game here, which was reestablishing herself and the Beaumont name and inflicting as much collateral damage on the new Brewery owners and operators as possible.

So this was her, inflicting a little collateral damage on Ethan—even if the dull throb that seemed to circle between her legs and up to her nipples felt like a punishment in its own right.

Okay, so it was a lot of collateral damage.

She realized she was holding her breath as she waited. Would he render their deal null and void? She didn't think so. She might not always be the best judge of men, but she was pretty sure Ethan wasn't going to claim sex behind tired old lines like "she led me on." There was something about him that was more honorable than that.

Funny. She hadn't thought of him as honorable before this moment.

But he was. He muttered something that sounded like a curse before he stalked out of her line of vision. She heard the bathroom door slam shut and exhaled.

The score was Frances: two and Ethan: one. She was winning.

She shifted on the bed. If only victory wasn't taking the shape of sexual frustration.

Frances had just stumbled on some sort of sporting event—basketball, maybe?—when Ethan threw the bathroom door open again. He stalked into the room in nothing but his trousers and a plain white T-shirt. He went over to the desk, set against the window, and opened his computer. "How long do you need to be here?" he asked in an almost-mean voice.

"That's open to discussion." She looked over at him. He was pointedly glaring at the computer screen. "I obviously didn't bring a change of clothing."

That got his attention. "You wouldn't stay the night, would you?"

Was she wrong, or was there a note of panic in his voice? She pushed herself into a sitting position, tucking her feet under her skirt. "Not yet, I don't think. But perhaps by next week, yes. For appearances."

He stared at her for another tight moment and then ground the heels of his palms into his eyes. "This seemed like *such* a good idea in my head," he groaned.

She almost felt bad for him. "We'll need to have dinner in public again tomorrow night. In fact, at least four or five nights a week for the next two weeks. Then I'll start sleeping over and—"

"Here?" He made a show of noticing there was only one bed and a pullout couch. "Shouldn't I come to your place?"

"Um, no." The very last thing she needed was to parade her fake intended husband through the Beaumont mansion. God only knew what Chadwick would do if he caught wind of this little scheme of hers. "No, we should stick to a more public setting. The hotel suits nicely."

"Well." He sagged back in his chair. "That's the evenings. And during the day?"

She considered. "I'll come to the office a couple of times a week. We'll say that we're discussing the sale of the antiques. On the days I don't stop by, you should have Delores order flowers for me."

At that, Ethan cocked an eyebrow. "Seriously?"

"I like flowers, and you want to look thoughtful and attentive, don't you?" she snapped. "Fake marriage or not, I expect to be courted."

"And what do I get out of this again?"

"A wife." A vein stood out on his forehead, and she swore she could see the pulse in his massive neck even at this distance. "And an art gallery." She smiled widely.

The look he shot her was hard enough that she shrank back.

"So," she said, unwilling to let the conversation drift back to sex just quite yet. "Tell me about this successful long-distance relationship that we're modeling our marriage upon."

"What?"

"You said at dinner that you've seen long-distance relationships work quite well. Personally, I've never seen any relationship work well, regardless of distance."

The silence between them grew. In the background, she heard the whistles and buzzers of the game on the TV.

"It's not important," he finally said. "So, fine. We won't exactly be long-distance for the next two weeks. Then we get married. Then what?"

"Oh, I imagine we'll have to keep up appearances for a month or so."

"A *month*?"

"Or so. Ethan," she said patiently. "Do you want this

to be convincing or not? If we stop being seen together the day after we tie the knot, no one will believe it wasn't a publicity stunt."

He jumped out of his chair and began to pace. "See—when I said long-distance, I didn't actually anticipate being in your company constantly."

"Is that a bad thing?" She batted her eyes when he shot her an incredulous look.

"Only if you keep kissing me like you did in the elevator."

"I can kiss you less, but we have to spend time together." She shifted so she was cross-legged on the bed. "Can you do that? At the very least, we have to be friends."

The look he gave her was many things—perhaps angry, horny—but "friendly" was not on the list.

"If you can't, we can still call it off. A night of wild indiscretion, we'll both 'no comment' to the press—it's not a big deal." She shrugged.

"It's a huge deal. If I roll into the Brewery after everyone thinks I had a one-night stand with you and then threw you to the curb, they'll hang me up by my toenails."

"I am rather well liked by the employees," she said, not a little smugly. "Which is why you thought up this plan in the first place, is it not?"

He looked to the ceiling and let out another muttered curse. "Such a good idea," he said again.

"Best laid plans of mice and men and all that," she agreed. "Well?"

He did a little more unproductive pacing, and she let him think. Honestly, she didn't know which way she wanted him to go.

There'd been the heat that had arced between them, heat that had melted her in places that hadn't been properly melted in a very long time. She'd kissed before, but Ethan's mouth against hers—his body against hers—

She needed the money. She needed the fresh start that an angel investor could provide. She needed to feel the power and prestige that went with the Beaumont name—or had, before Ethan had taken over. She needed her life back. And if she got to take the one man who embodied her fall from grace down a couple of pegs, all the better.

It was all at her fingertips. All she had to do was get married to a man she'd promised not to love. How hard could that be? She could probably even have sex with him—and it would be *so* good—without love ever entering into the equation.

"No more kissing in the elevator."

"Agreed." At least, that's what she said. She would be lying if she didn't admit she was enjoying the way she'd so clearly brought him to his knees with desire.

"What do people do in this town on a Sunday afternoon?"

That was a yes. She'd get her funding and make a few headlines and be back on top of the world for a while.

"I'll take it easy on you tomorrow—we need to give the gossip time to develop."

He shot her a look and, for the first time since dinner, smiled. It appeared to be a genuine smile even. It set off his strong chin and deep eyes nicely. Not that she wanted him to know that. "Should I be worried that you know this much about manipulating the press?"

She brushed that comment aside. "It comes with the territory of being a Beaumont. I'll leave after this game is over, and then I'll stop by the office on Monday. Deal?"

"Deal."

They didn't shake on it. Neither of them, it seemed, wanted to tempt fate by touching again.

Seven

"Becky? You're not going to believe this," Frances said as she stood in front of her closet, weighing the red evening gown versus something more…restrained. She hated being restrained, but on her current budget, it was a necessary concession.

"What? Something good?"

Frances grinned. Becky was easily excitable. Frances was pretty sure she could hear her friend bouncing up and down. "Something great. I found an investor."

There was some screaming. Frances held the phone as far away from her face as she could until the noise died down. She flicked through the hangers. She needed something sexy that didn't look as if she was trying too hard. The red gown would definitely be trying too hard for a Monday at the office. "Still with me?"

"Ohmygosh—this is so exciting! How much were they willing to invest?"

Frances braced herself for more screaming. "Up to five."

"Thousand?"

"Million." She immediately jerked the phone away from her head, but there was no sound. She cautiously put it back to her ear. "Becky?"

"I—it—what? I heard you wrong," she said with a nervous laugh. "I thought you said…"

"Million. Five million," Frances repeated, her fingers landing on her one good suit—the Escada. It was a conservative cut—at least by her standards—with a formfitting pencil skirt that went below her knee and a close-cropped jacket with only a little peplum at the waist.

It was the color, however—a warm hot pink—that made her impossible to miss.

Oh—this would be perfect. All business but still dramatic. She pulled it out.

"What—how? *How?*" Frances had never heard Becky this speechless before. "Your brothers?"

Frances laughed. "Oh no—you know Chadwick cut me off after the last debacle. This is a new investor."

There was a pause. "Is he cute?"

Frances scowled—not that Becky could see it, but she did anyway. She did not like being predictable. "No." And that wasn't a lie.

Ethan was *not* cute. He existed in the space between handsome and gorgeous. He wasn't pretty enough to be gorgeous—his features were too rough, too masculine. But handsome—that wasn't right, either. He exuded too much raw sexuality to be handsome.

"Well?" Becky demanded.

"He's…nice."

"Are you sleeping with him?"

"No, it's not like that. In fact, sex isn't even on the table." Her mind oh so helpfully provided a mental picture that completely contradicted that statement. She could see it now—Ethan bending her over a table, yanking her skirt up and her panties down and—

Becky interrupted that thought. "Frannie, I just don't want you to do something stupid."

"I won't," she promised. "But I have a meeting with

him tomorrow morning. How quickly can you revise the business plan to accommodate a five-million-dollar investment?"

"Uh… Let me call you back," Becky said.

"Thanks, Becks." Frances ended the call and fingered the fine wool of her suit. This wasn't stupid, really. This was…marriage with a purpose. And that purpose went far beyond funding an art gallery, although that was one part of it.

This was about putting the Beaumonts back in control of their own destiny. Okay, this was about putting one Beaumont—Frances—back in control of her destiny. But that still counted for a lot. She needed to get over this slump she was in. She needed her name to mean something again. She needed to feel as if she'd done something for the family honor instead of being a deadweight.

Marrying Ethan was the means to a bunch of different ends. That was all.

Those other men who'd proposed, they'd wanted what she represented, too—the Beaumont name, the Beaumont fortune—but they'd never wanted her. Not the real her. They had wanted the illusion of perfection she projected. They wanted her to look good on their arm.

What was different about Ethan? Well, he got points for being up front about his motivations. Nothing couched in sweet words about how special she was or anything. Just a straight-up negotiation. It was refreshing. Really. She didn't want anything sweet that was nothing but a lie. She didn't want him to try and make her love him.

She had not lied. She would not love him.

That was how it had to be.

"Delores," Frances said as she swept into the reception area. "Is Ethan—I mean, Mr. Logan—in?" She tried to blush at the calculated name screw-up, but she wasn't sure she could pull it off.

Delores shot her an unreadable glance over the edge of her glasses. "Had a good weekend, did we?"

Well. That was all the confirmation Frances needed that the stunt she'd pulled back in the hotel had done exactly as she'd intended. People had noticed, and those people were talking. Of course, there'd been some online chatter, but Delores wasn't the kind of woman who existed on social media. If she'd heard about the "date," then it was a safe bet the whole company knew all the gritty details.

"It was lovely." And that part was not calculated at all. Kissing Ethan had, in fact, been quite nice. "He's not all bad, I don't think."

Delores snorted. "Just bad enough?"

"Delores!" This time, her blush was more unplanned. Who knew the older lady had it in her?

"Yes, he's in." Delores's hand hovered near the intercom.

"Oh, don't—I want to surprise him," Frances said.

As she swept open the massive oak door, she heard Delores say, "Oh, we're all surprised," under her breath.

Ethan was sitting at her father's desk, his head bent over his computer. He was in his shirtsleeves, his tie loosened. When she flung the door open, his head popped up. But instead of looking surprised, he looked pleased to see her. "Ah, Frances," he said, rising to his feet.

None of the strain that she'd inflicted on him two days ago showed on his face now. He smiled warmly as he came around the desk to greet her. He did not, she noticed, touch her. Not even a handshake. "I was expecting you at some point today."

Despite the lack of physical contact, his eyes took in her hot-pink suit. She did a little twirl for him, as if she needed his approval when they both knew she didn't. Still, when he murmured, "I'm beginning to think the black dress is the most conservative look you have," she felt her cheeks warm.

For a second, she thought he was going to lean forward and kiss her on the cheek. He didn't. "You would not be wrong." She waltzed over to the leather love seats and spread herself out on one. "So? Heard any of the chatter?"

"I've been working. Is there chatter?"

Frances laughed. "You can be adorably naive. Of course there's chatter. Or did Delores not give you the same look she gave me?"

"Well…" He tugged at his shirt collar, as if it'd suddenly grown a half size too small. "She was almost polite to me this morning. But I didn't know if that was because of us or something else. Maybe she got lucky this weekend."

Unlike some of us. It was the unspoken phrase on the end of that statement that was as loud as if he'd pronounced the words.

She grinned and crossed her legs as best she could in a skirt that tight. "Regardless of Delores's private life, she's aware that we had an intimate dinner. And if Delores is aware of it, the rest of the company is, as well. There were several mentions on the various social media sites and even a teaser in the *Denver Post* online."

His eyes widened. "All of that from one dinner, huh? I am impressed."

She shrugged, as if this were all just another day at the office. Well, for her, it sort of was. "Now we're here."

He notched an eyebrow at her. "And we should be doing…what?"

She slipped the computer out of her bag. "You have a choice. We can discuss art or we can discuss art galleries. I've worked up a prospectus for potential investors."

Ethan let out a bark of laughter. "I've got to stop being surprised by you, don't I?"

"You really do," she agreed demurely. "In all honesty, I'm not that shocking. Not compared to some of my siblings."

"Tell me about them," he said, taking a perfectly safe seat to her right—not within touching distance. "Since we'll be in-laws and all that. Will I get to meet them?"

"It does seem unavoidable." She hadn't really considered the scene where the Beaumonts welcomed Ethan into the family fold with open arms. "I have nine half siblings from my father's four marriages. My older brothers are aware of other illegitimate siblings, but it's not unreasonable that there are more out there." She shrugged, as if that were normal.

Well, it was for her, anyway. Marriages, children, more children—and love had nothing to do with it.

Maybe there'd been a time, back when she was still a little girl who'd twirled in this office, when she'd been naive and innocent and had thought that her father loved her—and her brothers, their mother. That they were a family.

But then there'd been the day… She'd known her parents weren't happy. It was impossible to miss, what with all the screaming, fights, thrown dishes and slammed doors.

And it'd been Donut Friday and she'd been driven to the office with all those boxes and had bounced into the office to see her daddy and found him kissing someone who wasn't her mommy.

She'd stood there, afraid to yell, afraid to not yell—or cry or scream or do something that gave voice to the angry pain that started in her chest and threatened to leak out of her eyes. In the end, she'd done nothing, just like Owen, the driver who'd brought her and was carrying the donuts. Nothing to let her father know how much it hurt to see his betrayal. Nothing to let her mother know that Frances knew now what the fights were about.

But she knew. She couldn't un-know it, either. And

if she called her daddy on it—asked why he was kissing the secretary who'd always been so nice to Frances—she knew her father might put her aside like he'd put her mother aside.

So she said nothing. She showed nothing. She handed out donuts on that day with the biggest, best smile she could manage. Because that's what a Beaumont did. They went on, no matter what.

Just like now. So what if Ethan would eventually have to meet the family? So what if her siblings would react to this marriage with the same mix of shock and horror she'd felt when she'd walked in on her father that cold gray morning so long ago? She would go on—head up, shoulders back, a smile on her face. Her business failed? She couldn't get a job? She'd lost her condo? She'd been reduced to accepting the proposal of a man who only wanted her for her last name?

Didn't matter. Head up, shoulders back, a smile on her face. Just like right now. She called up the prospectus that Becky had put together yesterday in a flurry of excited phone calls and emails. Becky was the brains of the operation, after all—Frances was the one with the connections. And if she could deliver Ethan gift wrapped...

An image of him in nothing but a strategically placed bow popped before her. Christmas might be long gone, but there'd be something special about unwrapping *him* as a present.

She shook that image from her mind and handed the computer over to Ethan. "Our business plan."

He scrolled through it, but she got the distinct feeling he was barely looking at it. "Four wives?"

"Indeed. As you can see, my partner, Rebecca Rosenthal, has mocked up the design for the space as well as a cost-benefit analysis." She leaned over to click on the next tab. "Here's a sampling of the promotion we have planned."

"Ten siblings? Where do you fall in that?"

"I'm fifth." For some reason, she didn't want to talk about her family.

Detailing her father's affairs and indiscretions in this, his former office, felt wrong. This was where he'd been a good father to her. Even after she'd walked in on him cheating with his secretary, when she hadn't thrown a fit and hadn't tattled on him, he'd still doted on her when she was here. The next Donut Friday, she remembered, he'd had a pretty necklace waiting for her, and once again she'd been Daddy's girl for a few special minutes each week.

She didn't want to sully those memories. "Chadwick and Phillip with my father's first wife, Matthew and then Byron and me—we're twins—with his second wife." She hated referring to her mother by that number, as if that's all Jeannie had contributed. Wife number two, children three, four and five.

"You have a twin?" Ethan cut in.

"Yes." She gave him humorous. look. "He's very protective of me." She did not mention that Byron was busy with his new wife and son. Better to let him worry about how her four older brothers would deal with him if he crossed a line.

Ethan's eyebrows jumped up. "And there were five more?"

"Yup. Lucy and Harry with my father's third wife. Johnny, Toni and Mark with his fourth. The younger ones are in their early twenties, for the most part. Toni and Mark are still in college and, along with Johnny, they all still live at the Beaumont mansion with Chadwick and his family." She rattled off her younger siblings' names as if they were items to be checked off a list.

"That must have been…interesting, growing up in that household."

"You have no idea." She made light of it, but *interesting* didn't begin to cover it.

She and Byron had been in an odd position in the household, straddling the line between the first generation of Hardwick Beaumont's sons and the last. Being five years older than she and Byron, Matthew was Chadwick and Phillip's contemporary. And since Matthew was their full brother, Byron and Frances had grown closer to the two older Beaumont brothers.

But then, her first stepmother—May, the not-evil one— had harbored delusional fantasies about how Frances and May's daughter, Lucy, would be the very best of friends, a period of time that painfully involved matching outfits for ten-year-old Frances and three-year-old Lucy. Which had done the exact opposite of what May intended—Lucy couldn't stand the sight of Frances. The feeling was mutual.

And the youngest ones—well, they'd been practically babies when Frances was a teenager. She barely knew them.

They were all Beaumonts, and, by default, that meant they were all family.

"What about you? Any strings of siblings floating around?"

Ethan shook his head. "One younger brother. No stepparents. It was a pretty normal life." Something in the way he said it didn't ring true, though.

No stepparents? What an odd way to phrase it. "Are you close? With your family, I mean." He didn't answer right away, so she added, "Since they'll be my in-laws, too."

"We keep in touch. I imagine the worst-case scenario is that my mother shows up to visit."

We keep in touch. What was it he'd said, about longdistance relationships working?

It was his turn to change the subject before she could

drill for more information. "You weren't kidding about an art gallery, were you?"

"I am *highly* qualified," she repeated. This time, her smile was more genuine. "We envision a grand space with enough room to highlight sculpture and nontraditional media, as well as hosting parties. As you can see, a five-million-dollar investment will practically guarantee success. I think that, as a grand opening, it would be ideal to host a showing of the antiques in this room. I don't want to auction off these pieces. Too impersonal."

He ignored the last part and focused instead on the one part Frances would have preferred to gloss over. "Practically?" He glanced at her. "What kind of track record do you have with these types of ventures?"

Frances cleared her throat as she uncrossed and recrossed her legs before leaning toward Ethan. Her distraction didn't work this time. At least, not as well. His gaze only lingered on her legs for a few seconds. "This is a more conservative investment than my last ventures," she said smoothly. "Plus, Rebecca is going to be handling more of the business side of the gallery—that's her strong suit."

"You're saying you won't be in charge? That doesn't seem like you."

"Any good businesswoman knows her limitations and how to compensate for them."

His lips quirked up into a smile. "Indeed."

There was a knock at the door. "Come in," Ethan said. Frances didn't change her position. She wasn't exactly sitting in Ethan's lap, but her posture indicated that they were engaged in a personal discussion.

The door opened and what looked like two-dozen red roses walked into the room. "The flowers you ordered, Mr. Logan." Delores's voice came from behind the blooms. "Where should I put them?"

"On the table here." He motioned toward the coffee

table, but Delores couldn't see through that many blooms, so she put them on the conference table instead.

"That's a lot of roses," Frances said in shock.

Delores fished the card out of the arrangement and carried it over to her. "For you, dear," she said with a knowing smile.

"That'll be all, Delores. Thank you," Ethan said. But he was looking at Frances as he said it.

Delores smirked and was gone. Ethan stood and carried the roses over to the coffee table while Frances read the note.

Fran—here's to more beautiful evenings with a beautiful woman—E.

It hadn't been in an envelope. Delores had read it, no doubt. It was thoughtful and sweet, and Frances hadn't expected it at all.

With a sinking feeling in her stomach, Frances realized she might have underestimated Ethan.

"Well?" Ethan said. He sounded pleased with himself.

"Don't call me Fran," she snapped. Or she tried to. It came out more as a breathless whisper.

"What should I call you? It seems like a pet name would be the thing. Snoogums?"

She shot him a look. "I thought I said you should send me flowers when I didn't come to the office. Not when I was already here."

"I always send flowers after a great first date with a beautiful woman," he replied. He sounded sincere about it, which did not entirely jibe with the way he'd acted after she'd left him hanging.

In all honesty, it did sound sweet, as if the time they'd spent together had been a real date. But did that matter?

So what if this was a thoughtful gesture? So what if it

meant he'd been paying attention to her when she'd said she liked flowers and she expected to be courted? So what if the roses were gorgeous? It didn't change the fact that, at its core, this was still a business transaction. "It wasn't a great date. You didn't even get lucky."

He didn't look offended at this statement. "I'm going to marry you. Isn't that lucky enough?"

"Save it for when we're in public." But as she said it, she buried her nose in the roses. The heady fragrance was her favorite.

It'd been a while since anyone had sent her flowers. There was a small part of her that was more than a little flattered. It was a grand gesture—or it would have been, if it'd been sincere.

Honest? Yes. Ethan was being honest with her. He'd been totally up front about the reasons behind his interest in her.

But his attention wasn't sincere. These were, if possible, the most insincere roses ever. Just all part of the game—and she had to admit, he was playing his part well.

The thought made her sadder than she'd thought it might. Which was ridiculous. Sincerity was just another form of weakness that people could use to exploit you. Her mother had sincerely loved her father, and see where that had gotten her? Nowhere good.

The corners of Ethan's eyes crinkled, as if her less-than-gracious response amused him. "Fine. Speaking of, when would you like to be seen together in public again?"

"Tomorrow night. Mondays are not the most social day of the week. I think the roses today will accomplish everything we want them to."

"Dinner? Or did you have something else in mind?"

Did he sound hopeful? "Dinner is good for now. I'm keeping my eyes open for an appropriate activity this weekend."

He nodded, as if she'd announced that the sales projections for the quarter were on target. But then he stood and handed her computer back to her. As he did so, he leaned down and whispered, "I'm glad you liked the roses," in her ear. And, damn it all, heat flushed her body.

She tilted her head up to him. "They're beautiful," she murmured. There was no audience for this, no crowd to guess and gossip. Here, in the safety of this office, there was only him and her and dozens of honest roses.

He was close enough to kiss—more than close enough. She could see the golden tint to his brown eyes that made them lighter, warmer. He had a faint scar on the edge of his nose and another one on his chin. Football injuries or brawls? He had the body of a brawler. She'd felt that for herself the other night.

Ethan Logan was a big, strong man with big, strong muscles. And he'd sent her flowers.

She could kiss him. Not for show but for herself. She was going to marry him, after all. Shouldn't she get something out of it? Something beyond an art gallery and a restored sense of family pride?

His fingers slid under her chin, lifting her face to his. His breath was warm on her cheeks. Many things were warm at this point.

Not for the Beaumonts. Not for the gallery. Just for her. Ethan was just for *her*.

They held that pose as Frances danced right up to the line of kissing Ethan because she wanted to. But she didn't cross it. And after a moment, he relinquished his hold on her. But the warmth in his eyes didn't dim. He didn't act as if she'd rejected him.

Instead, he said, "You're welcome."

And that?

That was sincere.

Oh, hell.

Eight

First thing Tuesday morning, Ethan had Delores order lilies and send them to Frances. Roses every day felt too clichéd and he'd always liked lilies, anyway.

"Any message?" the old battle-ax asked. She sounded smug.

Ethan considered. The message, he knew, was as much for Delores's loose lips as it was for Frances. And no matter what Frances said, they needed pet names for each other. "Red—until tonight. E."

Delores snorted. "Will do, boss. By the way..."

Ethan paused, his hand on the intercom switch. *Boss?* That was the most receptionist-like thing Delores had said to him yet. "Yes?"

"The latest attendance reports are in. We're operating at full capacity today."

A sense of victory flowed through him. After four days, the implied Beaumont Seal of Approval was already working its magic. "I'm glad to hear it."

He switched off the intercom and stared at it for a moment. But instead of thinking about his next restructuring move, his thoughts drifted back to Frances.

She was going to kill him for the Red bit; he was reasonably confident about that. But there'd been that moment yesterday where he'd thought all her pretense had fallen away. She'd been well and truly stunned that he'd had flowers delivered for her. And in that moment, she'd seemed...vulnerable. All of her cynical world-weariness had fallen away, and she'd been a beautiful woman who'd appreciated a small gesture he'd made for her.

Marriage notwithstanding, she wasn't looking for anything long term. Neither was he. But that didn't mean the short term couldn't mean *something*, did it? He didn't need the fire to burn for long. He just needed it to burn bright.

He flipped the intercom back on. "Delores? Did you place that order yet?"

He heard her murmur something that sounded like, "One moment," before she said more clearly, "in process. Why?"

"I want to change the message. Red—" Then he faltered. "Looking forward to tonight. Yours, E." Which was not exactly a big change and he felt a little foolish for making it. He switched off the intercom again.

His phone rang. It was his partner at CRS, Finn Jackson. Finn was the one who pitched CRS to conglomerates. He was a hell of a salesman. "What's up?"

"Just wanted to let you know—there's activity," Finn began without any further introduction. "A private holding company is making noise about AllBev's handling of the Beaumont Brewery purchase."

Ethan frowned. "Link?"

"On its way." Seconds later, the email with the link popped up. Ethan scanned the article. Thankfully, it wasn't an attack on CRS's handling of the transition. However, this private holdings company, ZOLA, had written a letter stating that the Brewery was a poor strategic purchase for AllBev and they should dump the company—preferably on the cheap, no doubt.

"What is this?" he asked Finn. "A takeover bid? Is it the Beaumonts?"

"I don't think so," Finn replied, but he didn't sound convinced. "It's owned by someone named Zeb Richards—ring any bells for you?"

"None. How does this impact us?"

"This mostly appears to be an activist shareholder making noise. I'll keep tabs on AllBev's reaction, but I don't think this impacts you at the moment. I just wanted to keep you aware of the situation." Finn cleared his throat, which was his great tell. "You could ask your father if he knows anything."

Ethan didn't say a damned thing. His father? *Hell no.* He would never show the slightest sign of weakness to his old man because, unlike the Beaumonts, family meant nothing to Troy Logan. It never had, it never would.

"Or," Finn finally said, dragging out the word, "you could maybe see if anyone on the ground knows anything about this Zeb character?"

Frances. "Yeah, I can ask around. If you hear anything else, let me know. I'd prefer for the company not to be resold until we've fulfilled our contract. It'd look like a failure on the behalf of CRS—that we couldn't turn the company around fast enough."

"Agreed." With that, Finn hung up.

Ethan stared at his computer without seeing the files. He was just starting to get a grip on this company, thanks to Frances.

This ZOLA, whatever the hell it was, *felt* like it had something to do with the Beaumonts. Who else cared about this beer company? Ethan did a quick search. Privately held firm located in New York, a list of their successful investments—but not much else. Not even a picture of Zeb Richards. Something about it was off. This could easily be a shell corporation set up with the express purpose of wrestling the Brewery away from AllBev and back into Beaumont hands.

Luckily, Ethan happened to have excellent connections here on the ground. He'd have to tread carefully, though.

He needed Frances Beaumont. The production lines at full capacity today? That wasn't his keen management skills in action, as painful as it was to admit. That was all Frances.

But on the other hand…her sudden appearance happening so closely to this ZOLA business? It couldn't be a coincidence, could it?

Maybe it was; maybe it wasn't. One thing was for sure. He was going to find out *before* he married her and *before* he cut her a huge investment check.

He sent a follow-up message to his lawyers about protecting his assets and then glanced over Frances's art gallery plans again. He knew nothing about art, which was surprising, considering his mother was the living embodiment of "artsy-fartsy." So as an art space, it didn't mean much to him. But as a business investment?

It wasn't that he couldn't spot her the five million. He had that and much more in the bank—and that didn't count his golden-parachute bonuses and stock options. Restructuring corporations was a job that paid extremely well. It just felt…

Too familiar. Like he was hell-bent on replicating his parents' unorthodox marriage. And that wasn't what he wanted.

He pushed the thoughts of his all-business father and flighty mother out of his brain. He had a company to run, a private equity firm to investigate and a woman to woo, if people still did that. And above all that, tonight he had a date.

This really wasn't that different from what he normally did, Ethan told himself as he waited at the bar of some hip restaurant. He rolled into a new town, met a woman and did the wining-and-dining thing. He saw the sights, had a little fun and then, when it was time, he moved on. This was standard stuff for him.

Which did not explain why he was sipping his gin and tonic with a little more enthusiasm than the drink required. He was just…bracing himself for another evening of sexual frustration, that was all. Because he knew that, no matter what she was wearing tonight, he wouldn't be able to take his eyes off Frances.

Maybe it wouldn't be so bad if she were just another pretty face. But she wasn't. He'd have to sit there and look at her and then also be verbally pummeled by her sharp wit as she ran circles around him. She challenged him and pushed him to his very limits of self-control, and that was something he could honestly say didn't happen much. Oh, the women he'd seen in the past were all perfectly intelligent ladies, but they didn't see their role of temporary companion as one that included the kind of conversation that bordered on warfare.

But Frances? She was armed like a Sherman tank, and she had excellent aim. She knew how to take him out with a few well-chosen words and a tilt of her head. He was practically defenseless against her.

His only consolation—aside from her company—was that he'd managed to slip past her armor a few times.

Then Frances was there, framed by the doorway. She had on a thick white coat with a fur collar that was belted tightly at the waist and a pair of calf-high boots in supple brown leather. Her hair was swept into an elegant updo and—Ethan blinked. Did she have flowers in her hair? Lilies?

Perhaps the rest of the restaurant was pondering the same question because he would have sworn the whole place paused to note her arrival.

She spotted him and favored him with a small personal

smile. Then she undid the belt of her coat and let it fall off her shoulders.

This wasn't normal, the way he reacted to what had to be the calculated revelation of her body. Hell, it wasn't even that much of a reveal—she had on a slim brown skirt and a cream-colored sweater. The sweater had a sweetheart neckline and long sleeves. Nothing overtly sexual about her appearance tonight.

She was just a gorgeous woman. And she was headed right for him. The restaurant was so quiet he could hear the click of her heels on the parquet flooring as she crossed to the bar.

He couldn't take his eyes off her.

What if things were different? What if they'd met on different terms—him not trying to reconstruct her family's former company, her not desperate for an angel investor? Would he have pursued her? Well, that was a stupid question—of course he would have. She was not just a feast for the eyes. She was quite possibly the smartest woman he'd ever gone head-to-head with. He couldn't believe it, but he was actually looking forward to being demolished by her again tonight. Blue balls be damned.

He rose and greeted her. "Frances."

She leaned up on her tiptoes and kissed his cheek. "What," she murmured against his skin. "Not Red?"

He turned his head slightly to respond but just kissed her instead. He kissed her like he'd wanted to kiss her in his office the other day. The taste of her lips burned his mouth like those cinnamon candies his mother preferred—hot but sweet. And good. *So* good. He couldn't get enough of her.

And that was a problem. It was quickly becoming *the* problem. He was having trouble going a day or two without touching her. How was he supposed to make it a year in a sexless marriage?

She pulled away, and he let her. "Still trying to find the right name for you," he replied, hoping that how much she affected him didn't show.

"Keep trying." She cocked her head to one side. "Shall we?"

Ethan signaled for the hostess, who led them back to their private table. "How was your day, darling?" Frances asked in an offhand way as she accepted the menu.

The casual nature of the question—or, more specifically, the lack of sexual innuendo—caught him off guard. "Fine, actually. The production lines were producing today." She looked at him over the edge of her menu, one eyebrow raised. "And, yes," he said, answering the unspoken question. "I give you all the credit for that."

He wanted to ask about ZOLA and Zeb Richards, but he didn't. Maybe after they'd eaten—and shared a bottle of wine. "How about you?"

They were interrupted by the waitress, so it wasn't until after they'd placed their orders that she answered. "Good. We met with the Realtors about the space. Becky's very excited about owning the space instead of renting."

Ah, yes. The money he owed her. "Have you been monitoring the chatter, as you put it?"

At that, she leaned forward, a winning smile on her face. Ethan didn't like it. It wasn't real or true. It was a piece of armor, a shield in this game they were playing. She wasn't smiling for him. She was smiling for everyone else. "So far, so good," she purred, even though there was no one else who could have heard her. "I think this weekend, we should attend a Nuggets game."

He dimly remembered her watching a basketball game on Saturday when she'd been pointedly not sleeping with him. "Big fan?"

"Not really," she replied with a casual shrug. "But sports

fans drink a lot of beer. It'd signal our involvement to a different crowd and boost the chatter significantly."

All of that sounded fine in a cold, calculated kind of way. He found he didn't much care for the cold right now. He craved her heat.

It was his turn to lean forward. "And after that? I seem to recall you saying something about how you were going to start sleeping over this weekend. Of course, you're always welcome to do so sooner."

That shield of a smile fell away, and he knew he'd slipped past her defenses again. But the moment was short. She tilted her head to one side and gave him an appraising look. "Trying to change the terms of our deal again? For shame, Ethan."

"Are you coming back to the room with me tonight?"

"Of course." Her voice didn't change, but he thought he saw her cheeks pink up ever so slightly.

"Are you going to kiss me in the lobby again?"

Yes, she was definitely blushing. But it was her only tell. "I suppose you could always kiss me first. Just for a little variety."

Oh, he'd love to show her some variety. "And the elevator?"

"You *are* trying to change the terms," she murmured as she dropped her gaze. "We discussed that—at your request. There's no kissing in elevators."

He didn't respond. At the time, it'd seemed like the shortest path to self-preservation. But now? Now he wanted to push the envelope. He wanted to see if he could get to her like she was getting to him. "I like what you've done with the lily," he said, nodding toward where she'd worked the bloom into her hair. Because thus far, the flowers were by far the best way to get to her.

There was always a chance that she wasn't all that attracted to him—that the heat he felt when he was around her was a one-way street.

Damn, that was a depressing thought.

"They were beautiful," she said. And it could have easily been another too-smooth line.

But it wasn't.

"Not as beautiful as you are."

Before she could respond to that their food arrived. They ate and drank and made polite small talk disguised as sensual flirting.

"After the game, we'll have to deal with my family," she warned him over the lip of her second glass of wine after she'd pushed her plate away. "I'm actually surprised that my brother Matthew hasn't called to lecture me about the Beaumont family name."

Ethan was wrapped in the warm buzz of his alcohol. "Oh? That a problem?"

Frances waved her hand. "He's the micromanager of our public image. Was VP of marketing before you showed up. He did a great job, too."

She didn't say it as if she was intentionally trying to score a hit, but he felt a little wounded anyway. "I didn't fire him. He was gone before I got there."

"Oh, I know." She took another drink. "He left with Chadwick."

Ethan was pondering this information when someone said, "Frannie?"

At the name, Frances's eyes widened, and she sat bolt upright. She looked over Ethan's shoulder and said, "Phillip?"

Phillip? Oh, right. He remembered now. Phillip was one of her half brothers.

Oh, hell. Ethan was one sheet to the wind and about to meet a Beaumont.

Frances stood as a strikingly blond man came around

the table. He was holding the hand of a tall, athletic woman wearing blue jeans. "Phillip! Jo! I didn't expect to see you guys here."

Phillip kissed his sister on the cheek. "We decided it was time for our once-a-month dinner date." As the woman named Jo hugged Frances, Phillip turned a gaze that was surprisingly friendly toward Ethan. "I'm Phillip Beaumont. And you are?" He stuck out his hand.

Ethan glanced at Frances, only to find that both she and Jo were watching this interaction with curiosity. "I'm Ethan Logan," Ethan said, giving Phillip's hand a firm shake.

He tried to pull his hand back, but it didn't go anywhere. "Ah," Phillip said. His smile grew—at the same time he clamped down on Ethan's hand. "You're running the Brewery these days."

The strength with which Phillip had a hold on him was more than Ethan would have given him credit for. Ethan would have anticipated her brother to be someone pampered and posh and not particularly physically intimidating. But Phillip's grip spoke of a man who worked with his hands for a living—and wasn't afraid to use them for other purposes.

"Phillip manages the Beaumont Farm," Frances said, her voice slightly louder than necessary. Ah, that explained it. "He raises the Percherons. And this is Jo, his wife. She trains horses."

It was only then that Phillip let go of Ethan so Ethan could give Jo's hand a quick shake. "A pleasure, Ms. Beaumont."

To his surprise, Jo said, "Is it?" with the kind of smile that made no pretense of being polite. But she linked arms with Phillip and physically pulled him a step away.

"Would you like to join us?" Ethan offered, because it seemed like the sociable thing to do and also because he absolutely did not want Phillip Beaumont to catch a hint of fear. Ethan would act as though having his hot date with Frances suddenly crashed by an obviously overprotective older brother was the highlight of his night if it killed him.

And given the look on Phillip's face, it just might.

"No," Jo said. "That's all right. You both look like you're finishing up, anyway."

Phillip said, "Frannie, can I talk with you—in private?"

That was a dismissal if Ethan had ever heard one. "I'll be right back," he genially offered. This called for a tactical retreat to the men's room. "If you'll excuse me," he added to Frances.

"Of course," she murmured, nodding her head in appreciation.

As Ethan walked away, he heard nothing but chilly silence.

"What are you doing?" Phillip didn't so much say the words as hiss them. His fun-times smile never wavered, though.

In that moment Phillip sounded more like stuck-up Matthew than her formerly wild older brother. "I'm on a date. Same as you."

Beside her, Jo snorted. But she didn't say anything. She just watched. Sometimes—and not that Frances would ever tell her sister-in-law this—Jo kind of freaked her out. She was so quiet, so watchful. Not at all the kind of woman Frances had envisioned with Phillip.

Which was not a complaint. Phillip was sober now and, with Jo beside him, almost a new man.

A new man who'd tasked himself with making sure Frances toed the family line. *Ugh.*

"With the man who's running the Brewery? Are you drunk?"

"That is *such* a laugh riot, coming from you," she stiffly

replied. She felt Jo tense beside her. "Sorry." But she said it to Jo. Not to Phillip. "But no, thanks for asking, I'm not drunk. I'm not insane, and, just to head you off at the pass, I'm not stupid. I know exactly who he is, and I know exactly what I'm doing."

Phillip glared at her. "Which is *what*, exactly?"

"None of your business." She made damn sure to say it with her very best smile.

Phillip was not swayed. "Frannie, I don't know what you think you're doing here—either you're completely clueless and setting yourself up for yet another failure or—"

"And thank you for that overwhelming vote of confidence," she hissed at him, her best smile cracking unnaturally. "I liked you better when you were drunk. At least then you didn't assume I was an idiot like everyone else does."

"Or," Phillip went on, refusing to be sidetracked by her attack, "you think you're going to accomplish something at the Brewery." He paused, and when Frances didn't respond immediately to that spot-on accusation, his eyes widened. "What on earth do you think you're doing?"

"I don't see what it matters to you. You don't drink beer. You don't work at any brewery, old or new. You've got the farm, and you've got Jo. You don't need anything." He had his happy life now. He couldn't begrudge her this.

Phillip did grab her then, wrapping his hand around her upper arm. "Frannie—corporate espionage?"

"I'm just trying to restore the Beaumont name. You may not remember it, but our name used to mean something. And we lost that."

Unexpectedly, Phillip's face softened. "We didn't lose anything. We're still Beaumonts. You can't go back—why would you even want to? Things are better now."

If that wasn't the most condescending thing Phillip had

ever said to her, she didn't know what was. "Better for who? Not for me."

He was undaunted, damn him. "We've moved on—we *all* have. Chadwick and Matthew have their new business. Byron's back and happy. Even the younger kids are doing okay. None of us want the Brewery back, honey. If that's what you're trying to do here…"

A rush of emotions Frances couldn't name threatened to swamp her. It was what she wanted, but it wasn't. This was about *her*. She wanted Frances Beaumont back.

She turned to Jo, who'd been watching the entire exchange with unblinking eyes. "I'm sorry if this interrupted your night out. Ethan and I were almost done anyway."

"It's not a problem," Jo said. Frances couldn't tell if Jo was saying it to her husband or to Frances. Jo then slid her arm through Phillip's. "Let it be, babe."

Phillip gave his wife an apologetic look. "My apologies. I'm just surprised. I'd have thought…"

She knew what Phillip would have thought—and she knew what Chadwick and Matthew and even Byron would all be thinking, just as fast as Phillip could text them. Another Frances misadventure. "Trust me, okay?"

Phillip's gaze cut back over her shoulder. Even without looking, Frances could tell Ethan had returned. She could *feel* his presence. Warm prickles raised the hairs on the back of her neck as he approached.

Then his arm slid around her waist in an act that could only be described as possessive. Phillip didn't miss it, curse his clean-and-sober eyes. "Well. Logan, a pleasure to meet you. Frances…"

She could hear the unspoken *be careful* in his tone. She gave Jo another quick hug and Phillip a kiss on the cheek. Ethan's hand stayed on her lower back. "I'll come out soon," she promised, as if that was what their little chat had been about.

Phillip smirked at the dodge. But he didn't say anything else. He and Jo moved off to their own table.

"Everything okay?" Ethan said. His arm was firmly back around her waist and she wanted nothing more than to lean into him.

"Oh, sure." It wasn't a lie, but it wasn't the whole truth. For someone who'd been playing a game calculated on public recognition, Frances suddenly felt overexposed.

Ethan's fingertips tightened against her side, pulling her closer against his chest. "Do you want to go?"

"Yes."

Ethan let go of her long enough to fish several hundred-dollar bills out of his wallet, and then they were walking toward the front. He held her coat for her before he slid his own back on. Frances could feel the weight of Phillip's gaze from all the way across the room.

Why did she feel so…weird? It wasn't what Phillip thought. She wasn't being naive about this. She wasn't betraying the family name—she was rescuing it, damn it. She was keeping her friends—and family—close and her enemies closer, by God. That's all this was. There was nothing else to it.

Except…except for the way Ethan wrapped his strong arm around her and hugged her close as they walked out of the restaurant and into the bitterly cold night air. As they walked from the not-crowded sidewalk to the nearly empty parking lot, where he had parked a sleek Jaguar, he held her tighter still. He opened her door for her and then started the car.

But he didn't press. He didn't have to. All he did was reach over and take her hand in his.

When they arrived at the hotel, Ethan gave the keys to the valet, who greeted them both by name. They walked into the lobby, and this time, she did rest her head on his shoulder.

She shouldn't feel weird, now that someone in the family was aware of her…independent interests. Especially since it was Phillip, the former playboy of the family. She didn't need their approval, and she didn't want it.

But…she felt suddenly adrift. And what made it worse? Ethan could tell.

They didn't stop in the middle of the lobby and engage in heavy petting as planned. Instead, he walked her over to the elevator. While they waited, he lifted her chin with one gloved hand and kissed her.

Damn him, she thought even as she sighed into his arms. Damn Ethan all to hell for being exactly who he was—strong and tough and good at the game, but also honest and sincere and thoughtful.

She did not believe in love. She struggled with believing in *like*. Infatuation, yes—she knew that existed. And lust. Those entanglements that burned hot and fast and then fizzled out.

So no, this was not love. Not now, not ever. This was merely…fondness. She could be fond of Ethan, and he could return the sentiment. Perhaps they could even be friends. Wouldn't that be novel, being friends with her soon-to-be-ex husband?

The elevator doors pinged open, and he broke the kiss. "Shall we go up?" he whispered, his gaze never leaving hers as his fingers stroked her cheek. Why did he have to be like this? Why did he have to make her think he could care for her?

Why did he make her want to care for him?

"Yes," she said, her voice shaky. "Yes, let's."

They stepped onto the elevator.

The doors closed behind them.

Nine

Before she could sag back against the wall of the elevator, Ethan had folded her into his arms in what could only be described as a hug.

She sank into his broad and warm and firm chest. When was the last time she'd been hugged? Not counting when she went to visit her mother. Men wanted many things from her—sex, notoriety, sex, a crack at the Beaumont fortune and, finally, sex. But never something as simple as a hug, especially one seemingly without conditions or expectations.

"I'm fine," she tried to say, but her words were muffled by all his muscles.

His chest moved, as if he'd chuckled. "I'm sure you are. You are, without a doubt, the toughest woman I know."

Against her wishes, she relaxed into his embrace as they rode up and up and up. "You're just saying that."

"No, I'm not." He loosened his hold on her enough to look her in the eyes. "I'm serious. You've got some of the toughest, most effective armor I've ever seen a woman wear, and you hardly ever expose a chink."

Something stung at her eyes. She ignored it. "Save it for when we have an audience, Ethan."

Something hard flashed over his eyes. "I'm not saying this for the general public, Frances. I'm saying it because it's the truth." He traced his fingertips—still gloved—down the side of her face. "This isn't part of the game."

Her breath caught in her throat.

"But every so often," he went on, as if stunning her speechless was just par for the course, "something slips past that armor." She was not going to lean into his touch. Any more than she already had, that was. "It's subtle, but I can tell. You weren't ready for your brother just then. God knows I wasn't, either." His lips—lips she'd kissed—quirked into a smile. "I'd have loved to see what you'd done with him if you'd been primed for the battle."

"It's different when it's family," she managed to get out in a breathy whisper. "You have to love them even when they think you're making a huge fool of yourself."

She felt his body tense against hers. "Is that what he told you?"

"No, no—Phillip has far more tact than that," she told him. "But I don't think he approves."

The elevator slowed, and then the doors opened on Ethan's floor. Ethan didn't make a move to exit. "Does that bother you?"

She sighed. "Come on." It took more effort than she might have guessed to pull herself out of his arms, but when she held out her hand, he took it. They walked down the long hall like that, hand in hand. She waited while he got the door unlocked, and then they stepped inside.

This time, though, she didn't make a move for the remote. She just stood in the middle of his suite—the suite that she would be spending more and more time in. Spending the night in—until they got married. Then what? They'd have to get an apartment, wouldn't they? She couldn't live in a hotel suite. Not for a year. And she couldn't see moving Ethan into the Beaumont mansion with her. Just trying to picture that made her shudder in horror.

Good God, she was going to marry this man. In…a week and a half.

Ethan stepped up behind her and slid his hands around her waist. He'd shucked his gloves and coat, she saw as his fingers undid the belt at her waist. Then he removed her coat for her.

This wasn't an act. Or was it? He could still be working an angle, one in which his interests would best be served by making her think he was really a decent man, a good human being. It was possible. He could be looking to pump more information out of her. Looking to take another big chunk of power or money away from the Beaumonts. He could be building her up to drop her like a rock and put her in her place—especially after the stunt she'd pulled with Donut Friday.

Then his arms were around her again, pulling her back into him. "Does it bother you?" he asked again. "That they won't approve of this. Of us."

"They rarely approve of anything I do—but don't worry," she hurried to add, trying to speak over the catch in her voice. "The feeling is often mutual. Disapproval is the glue that holds the Beaumonts together." She tried to say it as if it were just a comical fact of nature—because it was.

But she felt so odd, so not normal, that it didn't come out that way.

"Is he your favorite brother? Other than your twin, I mean."

"Yes. Phillip threw the best parties and snuck me beers and…we were friends, I guess. We could do anything together, and he never judged me. But he's been sober for a while now. His wife helps."

"So he's not the same brother you knew." Ethan pulled the lily out of her hair and set it on the side table. Half of her hair fell out of the twist, and he used his fingers to unravel the rest.

"No, I guess not. But then, nothing stays the same. The only thing that never changes is change itself, right?"

She knew that better than anyone. Wasn't that how she'd been raised? There were no constants, no guarantees. Only the family name would endure.

Right up until it, too, had stopped meaning what it always had.

Unexpectedly, Ethan pressed his lips against her neck. "Take off your shoes," he ordered against her skin.

She did as he said, although she didn't know why. The old Frances wouldn't have followed an order from an admirer.

Maybe, an insidious little voice in the back of her head whispered, *maybe you aren't the same old Frances anymore*. And this quest, or whatever she wanted to call it, to undermine Ethan and strike a blow against the new owners of her family's brewery—all of that was to make her feel like the old Frances again. Even the art gallery was a step back to a place where she'd been more secure.

What if she couldn't go back there? What if she would never again be the redheaded golden girl of Denver? Of the Brewery? Of her family?

Ethan relinquished his hold on her long enough to peel back the comforter from the bed. Then he guided her down. "Scoot," he told her, climbing in after her.

She would have never done so, not back when she was at the top of her form. She would have demanded high seduction or nothing at all. Champagne. Wild promises. Diamonds and gems. Not this *fondness*, for God's sake.

He pulled the covers over them and wrapped his arm around her shoulder. She curled into his side, feeling warmer and safer by the moment. For some reason, it was what she needed. To feel safe from the winds of change that had blown away her prospects and her personal fortune. In Ethan's arms, she could almost pretend none of it had happened. She could almost pretend this was normal.

"What about you?" she asked, pressing her hand against his chest.

He covered her hand with his. Warm. Safe. "What about me?"

"You must be used to change. A new company and a new hotel in a new city every other month?" She curled her fingers into the crisp cotton of his shirt. "I guess change doesn't bother you at all."

"It doesn't feel like that," he said. "It's the same thing every time, with slightly different scenery. Hotel rooms all blend together, executive offices all look the same…"

"Even the women?"

The pause was long. "Yes, I guess you could say that. Even the women were all very similar. Beautiful, good conversationalists, cultured." He began to stroke her hair. "Until this time."

"This time?" Something sparked in her chest, something that didn't feel cynical or calculated. She didn't recognize what it was.

"The hotel is basically the same. But the company? I usually spend three to six months restructuring. I've already been here for three months and I've barely made any headway. The executive office—hell, the whole Brewery—is unlike any place I've ever worked before. It's not a sterile office building that's got the same carpeting and the same crappy furniture as every other office. It's like it's this…*thing* that lives and breathes on its own. It's not just real estate. It's alive."

"It's always been that way," she agreed, but she wasn't thinking about the Brewery or the antique furniture or the people who'd made it a second home to her.

She was thinking about the man next to her, the one

who'd just told her that women were as interchangeable as hotel rooms. Which was a cold, soulless thing to admit and also totally didn't match up with the way he was holding her.

"And?"

"And…" His voice trailed off as he wrapped his fingers more tightly around hers.

She swallowed. "The woman?"

For some reason, she needed to know that she wasn't like all the rest.

Please, she thought, *please say something I can believe. Something real and honest and sincere, even if it kills me.*

"The woman," he said, lifting her hand away from his chest and pressing a kiss to her palm, "the woman is unlike any other. Beautiful, a great conversationalist, highly cultured—but there's something else about her. Something that runs deeper."

Frances realized she was holding her breath, so she made herself breathe normally. Or as close to normal as she could get, what with her heart pounding as fast as it was. "You make her sound like a river."

"Then I'm not doing a very good job," he said with a chuckle. "I'm not used to whispering sweet nothings."

"They're not nothing." Her voice felt as if it were coming from somewhere far away.

His hand trailed down from her hair to her back, where he rubbed her in long, even strokes. "Neither are you."

She wasn't, was she? She was still Frances. Hell, in a few weeks, she wouldn't even be a Beaumont anymore. She'd be a Logan. And then after that… Well, nothing stayed the same, after all.

"We can call it off," he said, as if he'd been reading her mind.

She pushed herself up and stared down at him. *"What?"* Was he serious?

Or was this the real, honest, true thing she'd asked for? Because if this was it, she took it back.

"Nothing official has changed hands. No legal commitments have been made." She saw him swallow. He stared up at her with such seriousness that she almost panicked because the look on his face went so far beyond fond that she didn't know what to do. "If you want."

She sat all the way up, pushing herself out of what had been the safe shelter of his arms. She sat back on her heels, only vaguely aware that her skirt had twisted itself around her waist. "No. No! We can't end this!"

"Why not? Relationships end all the time. We had a couple of red-hot dates and it went nowhere." He tilted his head to the side. "We just walk away. No harm, no foul."

"*Just* walk away? We can't. *I* can't." Because that was the heart of the matter, wasn't it? She couldn't back out of this deal now. This was her ticket back to her old life, or some reasonable facsimile thereof. With Ethan's angel investment, she could get the gallery off the ground, she could get a new apartment and move out of the Beaumont mansion. She could go back to being Frances Beaumont.

He sat up, which brought their bodies into close proximity again. She didn't like being this aware of him. She didn't like the fact that she wanted to know what he'd look like without the shirt. She didn't want to like him. Not even a little.

He reached over and stroked her hair tenderly. She didn't want tenderness, damn it. She didn't want feelings. She wanted cutting commentary and wars of words and… She wanted to hate him. He was the embodiment of her family's failures. He was dismantling her second home piece by piece. He was using her for her familial connections.

And he was making it damned near impossible to hate him. Stupid tender fondness.

It only got worse when he said, "I'd like to keep seeing

you," as if he thought that would make it better when it only made everything worse. "I don't think it's an exaggeration to say that I haven't stopped thinking about you since the moment you offered me a donut. But we don't have to do this rush to the altar. We don't have to get married. Not if you'd like to change the deal. Since," he added with a wry smile, "things do change."

"But you need me," she protested, trying vainly to find some solution that would not lead to where she'd started—alone, living at the family home, broke, with no prospects. "You need *me* to make the workers like you."

His lips quirked up into a tender smile, and then he was closing the distance between them. "I need more than just that."

He was going to kiss her. He was being sweet and thoughtful and kind and he was going to kiss her and it was wrong. It was all wrong.

"Ethan," she said in warning, putting her hand on his chest and pushing lightly. "Don't do this."

He let her hold him back, but he didn't let go of her hair. He didn't let go of *her*. "Do what?"

"This—*madness*. Don't start to like me. I won't like you back." His eyes widened in shock. She dug deeper. "I won't love you."

Ever so slightly, his fingers loosened their hold on her hair. "You already said that."

"I meant it. Love is for fools, and I refuse to be one. Don't lower my opinion of you by being one, too." The words felt sharp on her tongue, as if she were chewing on glass.

Cruel to be kind, she told herself. If he got infatuated with her—if real emotions came into play—well, this whole thing would fall apart. This was not a relationship, not a real one. This was a business deal. They couldn't afford to forget that.

Well, she couldn't, anyway.

If she'd expected him to pull away, to be pissed at her blanket rejection, she was sorely disappointed. He did, in fact, lean back. And he did let his fingers fall away from her hair.

But he sat there, propped up on hotel pillows that were just like any other hotel pillows, and he smiled at her. A real smile, damn him. Honest and true.

"If you want out, that's fine," she pressed on. She would not be distracted by real emotions. "But don't take pity on me and don't like me, for God's sake. We had a deal. Don't patronize me by deciding what's best for me. If I want out of the deal, I'll tell you. In the meantime, I'll hold up my end of the bargain and you'll hold up yours—unless you've changed your mind?"

"I haven't," he said after a brief pause. His mouth was still slightly curved into a smile.

She wanted to wipe that smile off his face, but she couldn't think of a way to do it without kicking and screaming. So all she said was, "Fine."

They sat there for a few moments. Ethan continued to stare at her, as if he were trying to see into her. "Yes?" she demanded as she felt her face flush under his close scrutiny.

"The woman," he murmured in what sounded a hell of a lot like approval, "is a force unto herself."

Oh, she definitely took it back. She didn't want real or honest out of him. No tenderness and, for the love of everything holy, not a single hint of fondness.

She would not *like* him. She simply would not.

She had to nip this in the bud *fast*.

"Ethan," she said, baring her teeth in some approximation of a smile, "save it for when we're in public."

Ten

The next day, Ethan had Delores send a bird of paradise floral arrangement with a note that just read, "Yours, E." Then he sent Frances a text message telling her how much he was looking forward to seeing her again that night.

He wasn't surprised when she didn't respond. Not after the way she'd stalked out of his hotel room last night.

As hard as it was, he tried to put the events of the previous evening aside. He had work to do. The production lines were up to full speed. He checked in with his department heads and was stunned by the complete lack of pushback he got when he asked about head count and department budgets. A week ago, people would have been staring at the table or out the window and saying that the employees who had those numbers were out with the flu or on vacation or whatever lame excuse they assumed wouldn't be too transparent.

But now? After less than a week of having Frances Beaumont in his life, people were making eye contact and saying, "I've got those numbers," and smiling at him. Actually smiling! Even when a turnaround was going well, there weren't a lot of smiles in the process.

Then there was what happened at the end of the last meeting of the day. He'd been discussing the marketing budget in his office with the department managers. The men and women seated around the Beaumont conference table looked comfortable, as though they belonged there. For the briefest moment, Ethan was jealous of them. He didn't belong there, and they all knew it.

It was 4:45 and the marketing people were obviously ready to go home. Ethan wrapped things up, got the promises that he'd have the information he'd requested on his desk first thing in the morning and dismissed everyone.

"So, Mr. Logan," an older man said with a smile. Ethan thought his name was Bob. Larsen, maybe? "Are you going to get a donut on Friday?"

The room came to a brief pause, everyone listening for the answer. For what was quite possibly the first time, he grasped what Frances kept talking about when she said he should save it for the public.

Still, he had to say something. People were waiting for a reaction. More than that, they were waiting for the reaction that told them their trust in Ethan's decisions wasn't about to be misplaced. They were waiting for him to admit he was one of them.

"I hope she saves me a chocolate éclair this time," he said in a conspiratorial whisper. He didn't specify who "she" was. He didn't have to.

This comment was met with an approving noise between a chuckle and a hum. *Whew*, Ethan thought as people cleared out. At least he hadn't stuck his foot in it. Not like he had with Frances last night.

She'd been right. He *did* need her. If they walked away right now, whatever new, tenuous grip he had on this company would float away as soon as the last donut had been consumed. He'd gotten more accomplished in the past week than he had in three months, and, as much as it pained him to admit it, it had nothing to do with his keen managerial handling.

So why had he offered to let her out of their deal?

He didn't know the answer to that, except there'd been a chink in her armor and instead of looking like a worthy opponent, Frances had seemed delicate and vulnerable. There'd been this pull—a pull he wasn't sure he'd ever felt before—to take care of her. Which was patently ridiculous. She could take care of herself. Even if she hadn't seen fit to remind him of that fact, he knew it to be true.

But the look on her face after they'd left her brother behind...

Ethan hadn't lied. There were similarities between Frances and all his previous lady friends. Cultured, refined— the sort of woman who enjoyed a good meal and a little evening entertainment, both the kind that happened at the theater and in the hotel room.

So what was it about her that was so damn different?

It wasn't her name. Sure, her name was the starting point of this entire relationship, but Ethan was no sycophant. The Beaumont name was only valuable to him as long as it let him do his job at the Brewery. He had no desire to get in with the family, and Ethan had his own damn fortune, thank you very much.

Was it the fact that, for the first time in his life, he was operating with marriage in mind? Was that alone enough to merit this deeper...engagement, so to speak? He would be tied to Frances for the next calendar year. Maybe it was only natural to want to take care of the woman who would be his wife.

Not that he knew what that looked like. His father had certainly never taken care of his mother, aside from providing the funds for her to do whatever she liked. Troy Logan's involvement with the mother of his two sons was strictly limited to paying the bills. Maybe that was why his mother never stayed home for longer than a few months at a time. Troy Logan wasn't capable of deeper feeling, so

Wanda had sought out that emotional connection somewhere else. Anywhere else, really.

Ethan went to the private bathroom and splashed cold
water on his face. This wasn't supposed to be complicated,
not like his parents' relationship. This was cut-and-dried.
No messy emotions. Just playing a game with one hell of
an opponent who made him want to do things that were
completely out of character. No problem.

He checked his jaw in the mirror—maybe he wouldn't
shave before dinner tonight. As he was debating the mer-
its of facial hair, he heard his office door shut with a decent amount of force.

"Frances?" he called out. "Is that you?"

There was no response.

He unrolled his sleeves and slid his jacket back on.
The only other person who walked into his office without
being announced by Delores was Delores herself. Even if
it was near quitting time, he still needed to maintain his
professional image.

But as he walked back into his office, he knew it wasn't
Delores. Instead, a tall, commanding man sat in one of the
two chairs in front of the desk.

The man looked like Phillip Beaumont—until he gave
Ethan such an imperious glare that Ethan realized it wasn't
the same Beaumont.

He recognized that look. He'd seen it on the covers of
business magazines and in the *Wall Street Journal*. None
other than Chadwick Beaumont, the former CEO of the
Beaumont Brewery, was sitting in Ethan's office. The man
every single employee in this company wanted back.

Ethan went on high alert. Beaumont had, until this
very moment, been more of a ghost that Ethan had to
work around than an actual living man to be dealt with.
Yet here he was, months after Ethan had taken over. This

couldn't be a coincidence, not after the interaction with Phillip last night.

"I had heard," Beaumont began with no other introduction, "that you were going to tear this office out."

"It's my prerogative," Ethan replied, keeping his voice level. He had to give Beaumont credit—at least he hadn't said *my office*. "As I am the current CEO."

Beaumont tilted his head in acknowledgment.

"To what do I owe the honor?" Ethan asked, as if this were a social call when it was clearly anything but. He took his seat behind his desk, leaving both hands on the desktop, as if all his cards were on the table.

Beaumont did not answer immediately. He crossed his leg and adjusted the cuff of his pants. Which was to be expected, Ethan figured. Beaumont was a notoriously tough negotiator, much like his father had been.

Well, two could play at this game. Troy Logan had earned his reputation as a corporate raider during the 1980s the hard way. His name alone could make high-powered bankers turn tail and run. Ethan had learned at the feet of the master. If Beaumont thought he could gain something with this confrontation, he was going to be sorely disappointed.

While Beaumont tried to wait Ethan out, Ethan studied him.

Chadwick Beaumont—the scion of the Beaumont family—was taller and blonder than Frances or even his brother Phillip. His hair held just a shine of redness, whereas Frances's was all flame. There was enough similarity that, even if Ethan hadn't met Phillip the night before, he would have recognized the Beaumont features—the chin, the nose, the ability to command a room just by existing in it.

How had the company been sold away from this man? Ethan tried to recall. An activist shareholder had precipitated the sale. Beaumont had fought against it tooth and nail, but once the sale had been finalized, he'd packed up and moved on.

So, yeah—this wasn't about the company. This was about Frances.

Which Beaumont proved when he tried out something that was probably supposed to be a smile but didn't even come close. "You're making me look bad. Flowers every day? My wife is beginning to complain."

Ethan didn't smile back. "My apologies for that." He was not sorry. "That's not my intention."

One eyebrow lifted. "What are your intentions?"

Damn, Ethan had walked right into that one. "I'm sorry—is that any of your business?"

"I'm making it my business." The statement was made in a casual enough tone, but there was no missing the implicit threat. Beaumont tried to stare him down for a moment, but Ethan didn't buckle.

"Good luck with that."

Beaumont's eyes hardened. "I don't know what your game is, Logan, but you really don't know what you're getting into with her."

That might be a true enough observation, but Ethan wasn't about to concede an inch. "As far as I can tell, I'm getting into a relationship with a grown woman. Still don't see how that's any of your concern."

Beaumont shook his head slowly, as if Ethan had blundered into admitting he was an idiot. "Either she's using you or you're using her. It won't end well."

"Again, not your concern."

"It is my concern because this will be just another one of Frances's messes that I have to clean up after."

Ethan bristled. "You talk as if she's a wayward child."

Beaumont's glare bore into him. "You don't know her like I do. She's lost more fortunes than I can count. Keeping her out of the public eye is a challenge during the best of times. And you," he said, pointing his chin at Ethan, "are pushing her back into the public eye."

Ethan stared at Beaumont. Was he serious? But Chadwick Beaumont did not look like the kind of man who made a joke. Ever.

What had Frances said last night? "Don't patronize me by deciding what's best for me." Suddenly, that statement made sense. "Does she know you're here?"

"Of course not," Beaumont replied.

"Of course not," Ethan repeated. "Instead, you took it upon yourself to decide what was best not only for her but for me, as well." He gave his best condescending smile, which took effort. He did not feel like smiling. "You'll have to excuse me, but I'm trying to figure out what gives you the right to be such a patronizing asshole to a pair of consenting adults. Any thoughts on that?"

Beaumont gave him an even look.

"I suppose," Ethan went on, "that the only surprising thing is that you came alone to intimidate me, instead of with a herd of Beaumont brothers."

"We don't tend to travel in a pack," Beaumont said coolly.

"And I'm equally sure you didn't think you'd need any help in the intimidation department."

Beaumont's eyes crinkled a little at the corners, as if he might have actually found that observation amusing. "How's the Brewery doing?"

Ethan blinked at the subject change, but only once. "We're getting there. You cultivated an incredibly loyal staff. The ones that didn't follow you to your new company were not happy about the changes."

Beaumont tilted his head at the compliment. "I imagine not. When I took over after my father's death, there was a period of about a year where we verged on total collapse. Employee loyalty can be a double-edged sword."

Ethan didn't bother to hide his surprise. *"Really."*

Beaumont nodded. "The club of Beaumont Brewery CEOs is even more exclusive than the Presidents' Club. There are only two of us alive in the world. You're only the fifth person to helm this company." He stared down at Ethan, but the intimidation wasn't as overbearing. "It's not a position to be taken lightly."

Honest to God, Ethan had never thought about it in those terms. The companies he usually restructured had often gone through a new CEO every two or three years as part of their downhill spiral. He'd never been anything special, in terms of management. He'd waltzed in, righted the sinking ship and moved on—just another CEO in a long line of them. There'd been nothing for the other employees to be loyal to except a paycheck and benefits.

Beaumont was right. Frances was right. Everything about this place, these people—this was different.

"If you need any help with the company…"

Ethan frowned. Accepting help was not something he did, especially not when it came to his job.

Except for Frances, a silky voice in the back of his head whispered. It sounded just like her.

"Actually, I do have a question. Have you ever heard of ZOLA?"

"ZOLA?" Beaumont mouthed the word like it was foreign. "What's that?"

"A private holdings company. They're making noise about the Brewery. I think they're trying to undermine—well, I'm not sure who they're trying to undermine. Not you, obviously, since you're no longer the boss around here. But it could be my company, or it could be AllBev." He fought the urge to get up and pace. "Unless, of course, ZOLA is representing your interests."

"I have no interest in reclaiming the Brewery. I've

moved on." His gaze was level, and his hands and feet were calm. Beaumont was telling the truth, damn it.

"And the rest of your family?"

"I don't speak for the entire Beaumont family."

"I'll be sure and pass that information along to Frances."

Beaumont's eyes widened briefly in surprise at this barb. "Phillip has no interest in beer. Matthew is one of my executives. Byron has his own restaurant in our new brewery. The younger Beaumonts never had anything to do with the Brewery in the first place. And you seem to be in a position to form your own opinion of Frances's motivations."

Point. Ethan was quite proud that his ears didn't burn under that one. "I appreciate your input."

Beaumont stood and held out his hand. Ethan rose to shake it. "Good to meet you, Logan. Stop by the mansion sometime."

"Likewise. Anytime." He was pretty sure they were both lying through their teeth.

Beaumont didn't let go of his hand, though. If anything, his grip tightened down. "But be careful with Frances. She is not a woman to be trifled with."

Ethan cracked a real smile. As if anyone could trifle with Frances Beaumont and hope to escape with their dignity—or other parts—intact.

Still, this level of meddling was something new to Ethan. No wonder seeing her other brother last night had shaken her so badly. Ethan hadn't really anticipated this much peer pressure. He increased his grip right back. "I think she can take care of herself, don't you?"

He waited for Beaumont to make another thinly veiled threat, but he didn't. Instead, he dropped Ethan's hand and turned toward the door.

Ethan watched him go. If Beaumont had shown up here,

had anyone been designated to give Frances a talking-to? Hopefully she'd had her armor on.

Then Beaumont paused at the door. He turned back, his gaze sweeping the entirety of the room. Instead of another pronouncement about how they were members of the world's smallest club, he only gave Ethan a little grin that was somehow tinged with sadness before he turned and was gone.

Ethan got the feeling that Beaumont wouldn't come back to the Brewery again.

Ethan collapsed back into his chair. What the everloving hell was that all about, anyway? He still wasn't going to rule out Beaumont—any Beaumont—of having direct involvement with ZOLA. Including Frances. There were no such things as coincidences—she'd said so herself. Frances had waltzed into his life just as ZOLA had started making noise. There had to be a connection— didn't there? But if that connection didn't run through her brothers, what was it?

Frances. His thoughts always came back to her. He couldn't wait to see her at dinner tonight, but he got the feeling that she might need something a little more than a floral arrangement, if she'd gotten half the pushback Ethan had today.

He checked his watch. He had time to make a little side trip, if he didn't shave.

Hopefully Frances liked stubble.

Eleven

Frances was unsurprised to find Byron waiting for her when she got back to the mansion after a long day of going over real estate contracts.

"Phillip called you, didn't he?" she began, pushing past her twin brother on her way up to her room. She had a date tonight, and she was already on edge. This would be a great night to put on the red dress. That'd drive any thoughts of affection right out of Ethan's mind. He'd be nothing but a walking, talking vessel of lust, and that was something she knew how to deal with.

No more tenderness. End of discussion.

"He might have," Byron admitted as he followed her into her room.

She was about to tear Byron a new one when she saw the huge floral arrangement on her nightstand table. "Oh!"

The card read, "Yours, E." Of course it did.

Those two little words—a mere six letters—made her smile. Which was just another sign that she needed a shower and a stiff drink. Ethan was not hers any more than she was his. She would not like him.

It would be easier to hold that line if he could just stop being so damn perfect.

"George said you've gotten flowers every day this week."

Frances rolled her eyes. George was the chef at the mansion and far too close with Byron. "So?" she said, pointedly ignoring the massive arrangement of blooms. "It's not like I haven't gotten flowers before."

"From the guy running the Brewery?"

She leveled a tired look at Byron. It was not a stretch to pull it off. "Why are you here? Aren't you running a restaurant or something? It's almost dinnertime, you know."

Byron flopped down on her bed. "We haven't officially opened yet. If you're going to flounce all around town with this new guy, you could at least plan on stopping by next week when we open. We could use the boost."

Frances stalked to her closet and began wrenching the hangers from side to side. "Excuse me? I do not *flounce*, thank you very much."

"Look," Byron said, staring at her. "Phillip seemed to think you were making a fool of yourself. I'm sure Chadwick has been updated. But whatever's going on, you're more than capable of dealing with it. If you're seeing this guy because you like him, then I want to meet him. And if you're seeing him for some other reason…"

The jerk had the nerve to crack his knuckles.

"Oh, for God's sake, Byron," she huffed at him. "Ethan could break you in half. No offense."

"None taken," Byron said without a trace of insult in his voice. "All I'm saying is that Phillip asked me to talk to you, and I've done that. Consider yourself talked to."

She pulled out the red dress and hung it on the closet door. "Seriously?"

Byron looked at the dress and then whistled. "Damn, Frannie. You either really like him or…"

This was part of the game, wasn't it? Convincing other people that she did like Ethan a great deal. Even if those people were Byron. She wasn't admitting to anything, not really. Not as long as she knew the truth deep down inside.

"I do, actually." It was supposed to come out strong and powerful because she was a woman in control of the situation.

It didn't. And Byron heard the difference. He wrinkled his forehead at her.

She was suddenly talking far more than was prudent. But this was Byron, damn it. She'd been sharing with him since their time in the womb, for crying out loud. "I mean, I do like him. There's something about him that's not your typical multimillionaire CEO. But I don't like *like* him, you know?" Which did not feel like the most honest thing to say. Because she might like him, even if it were a really bad idea.

Wasn't that what had almost happened last night? She'd let her guard down, and Ethan had been right there, strong and kind and thoughtful and she almost liked him.

Byron considered her juvenile argument. "So if you don't like *like* him, you're busting out the red dress because…"

Her mouth opened, and she almost admitted to the whole plan—the sham wedding, the angel investment, how she'd originally agreed to the whole crazy plan so she could inflict a little collateral damage on the current owners of the Brewery. For the family honor. If anyone would understand, it'd be Byron. She could always trust her brother and, no matter how crazy the situation was, he'd always stand behind her. *Always*.

But…

She couldn't do it. She couldn't admit she was breaking out the red dress because this was all a game, with high-dollar, high-power stakes, and she needed to level the playing field after the disaster that had been last night.

Her gaze fell on the bird of paradise arrangement. It was beautiful and had no doubt cost Ethan a fortune. She couldn't admit to anyone that she might not be winning the game. Not to Byron. Not to herself.

She decided it was time for a subject change. "How's the family?" Byron had recently married Leona Harper, an old girlfriend who was, awkwardly, the daughter of the Beaumonts' nemesis. Leona and Byron had a baby boy and another baby on the way. "Any other news from Leon Harper?"

"No," Byron said. "I don't know what we're paying the family lawyers these days, but it's worth it. Not a peep." He dug out his phone and called up a picture. "Guess what?"

Frances squinted at the ultrasound. "It's a...baby? I already knew Leona was pregnant, you goof."

"Ah, but did you know this? It's a girl," he said, his voice brimming with love. It almost hurt Frances to hear it—and to know that was not what she had with Ethan. "We're going to name her Jeannie."

"After Mom?" Frances didn't have a lot of memories of her mother and father together—at least, not a lot of memories that didn't involve screaming or crying. But Mom had made a nice, quiet life for herself after Hardwick.

There had been times when Frances had been growing up in this mansion that she'd wanted nothing more than to move in with Mom and live a quiet life, too. Frances bore the brunt of the new wives' dislike. By then, her older brothers had been off at college or, in Byron's case, off in the kitchen. Frances was the one who'd been expected to make nice with the new wives and the new kids—and Frances was the one who was supposed to grin and bear it when those new wives felt the need to prove that Hardwick loved them more than he'd loved anyone else. Even his own daughter.

Love had always been a competition. Never anything more.

Until now, damn it. Chadwick had married his assistant,

and no matter which way Frances looked at it, the two of them seemed to be wildly in love. And Phillip—her former partner in partying—had settled down with Jo. He had never been the kind of man to stick to one woman, and yet he was devoted to Jo. Matthew had decamped to California to be with his new wife. And now this—Byron and his happy, perfect little family.

Were you winning the game if you were the only one still playing it?

Byron nodded. "Mom's going to move in with us."

Frances looked at him in surprise. "Really?"

"Dad was such a mess, and God knows Leona's parents are, too. But Mom can be a part of the family again. And we've got plenty of room," he added, as if that were the deciding factor. "A complete mother-in-law apartment. Percy adores her, and I think Leona is thrilled to have Mom around. She never had much of a relationship with her own mother, you know."

Frances, as jaded as she was, felt tears prick at her eyes. The one thing their mother had never gotten over was losing her sense of family when Hardwick Beaumont had steamrolled her in court. When she'd lost her game, she'd lost *everything*.

That wasn't going to be how Frances wound up. "Oh, Byron—Mom's going to be *so* happy."

"So," Byron said, standing and taking his phone back. "I know you. And I know that you are occasionally prone to rash decisions."

She narrowed her eyes at him. "Is this the part where I get to tell you to go to hell, so soon after that touching moment?"

But Byron held up his hands in surrender. "All I'm saying is, if you do something that some people *might* consider rash, just call Mom first, okay? She was there when

Matthew got married and when I got married. And I get dibs on walking you down the aisle."

Frances stared at him. *"What?"* Where had he gotten *that*? The impending wedding was something that she and Ethan had only discussed behind closed doors. No one else was supposed to have a clue.

No one but Byron, curse him. She'd never been able to hide anything from him for long, anyway, and he knew it. He gave her a wry smile and said, "You heard me. And come to the restaurant next week, okay? I'll save you the best table." He kissed her on the cheek and gave her shoulders a quick hug. "I've got to go. Take care, Frannie."

She stood there for several moments after Byron left. *Rash?* This wasn't rash. This was a carefully thought-out plan. A plan that did not necessarily include her mother watching her get married to Ethan Logan or having Byron—or any other brother—walk her down the aisle.

She didn't want her mother to think she'd found a happily-ever-after. Maybe she should call Mom and warn her that this whole thing wasn't real and it wouldn't last.

Frances found herself sitting on her bed, staring at the flowers. She was running out of room in here—the roses were on the dresser, the lilies on the desk. He didn't have to spend this much on flowers for her.

She plucked the card out and read it again. It didn't take long to process the two words. *Yours, E.*

She grinned as her fingertip traced the *E*. No, he was not particularly good at whispering—or writing—sweet nothings.

But he was hers, at least for the foreseeable future.

She needed to call her mom. And she would. Soon.

Right now, however, she had to get ready for a date.

Ethan knew the moment Frances walked into the restaurant. Not because he saw her do it, but because the entire place—including the busboy passing by and the bartender pouring a glass of wine—came to a screeching halt. There wasn't a sound, not even a fork scraping on a plate.

He knew before he even turned around that he wasn't going to make it. He wasn't going to be able to wall himself off from whatever fresh hell Frances had planned for him tonight. And what only made it worse? He didn't want to. God help him, he didn't want to.

While he finished his whiskey he took a moment to remind himself that part of the deal was that sex was not part of the deal. It didn't matter if she were standing there completely nude—he would give her his present and take her up to his hotel room and lock himself in the bathroom if he had to. He'd control himself. He'd never succumbed to wild passion before. Now was not the time to start.

After a long, frozen moment, everyone moved again. Ethan took a deep breath and turned around.

Oh, Jesus. She was wearing a strapless fire-engine-red dress that hugged every curve. And as good as she looked, all he wanted to do was strip that dress off her and see the real her, without armor—or anything else—on.

Even across the dim restaurant, he saw her smile when their eyes met. She did not like him, he reminded himself. That smile was for public consumption, not for him. But damned if it didn't make him smile back at her.

He got off his stool and went to meet her. He knew he needed to say things—for the diners who were all not so subtly listening in. He needed to compliment Frances's dress and tell her how glad he was to see her.

He couldn't get his stupid mouth to work. Even as part of his brain knew that was the whole point of that dress, he couldn't fight it.

He couldn't fight her.

So instead of words, he did the next best thing—he pulled her into his arms and kissed her like he'd been thinking of doing all damn day long. And it wasn't for the viewing public, either.

It was for her. All for her.

Somehow, he managed to pull away before he slid his hands down her back and cupped her bottom in the middle of the restaurant. "I missed you today," he whispered as he touched his forehead to hers.

"Did you?"

Maybe it was supposed to sound dismissive, but that's not how it hit his ears. Instead, she sounded as if she couldn't quite believe he was being sincere—but she wanted him to be.

"I did. Our table's ready." He took her hand in his and led her to the waiting table. After they were seated, he asked, "Anything interesting happen today?"

She arched an eyebrow at him. "Yes, actually. My twin, Byron, came to see me."

"Oh?" Had it been the same kind of visit he'd gotten from Chadwick?

Frances was watching him closely. "His new restaurant opens next week. He'd appreciate it if we could put in an appearance. Apparently, we're great publicity right now."

"Which was the plan," he said, more to remind himself than her. Because he had to stick to that plan, come hell or high water.

She leaned forward on her elbows, her generous cleavage on full display. He felt his pulse pick up a notch. "Indeed. You? Anything interesting today?"

"A few things," he tried to say casually. "Everyone at the Brewery is waiting to see if you bring me my very own donut this Friday."

A dazzling—and, he hoped, genuine—smile lit up her face. "Oh, really? I guess I should plan on coming, then?" Her tone was light and teasing.

This was what he'd missed today. She could talk circles

around him, and all he could do was keep up. He reached over and cupped her cheek in his hand, his thumb stroking her skin.

She leaned into his touch—a small movement that no one else could see. It was just for him, the way she let him carry a little of her weight. Just for him, the way her eyelashes fluttered. "I requested a chocolate éclair."

"Maybe I'll bring you a whole box, just to see what they say."

She would not like him. He should not like her.

But he did, damn it all. He liked her a great deal.

He didn't want to tell her the other interesting thing. He didn't want to watch her armor snap back into place at the mention of one of her brothers. Hell, for that matter, he didn't really want to be sitting in this very nice restaurant. He wanted to be someplace quiet, where they could be alone. Where her body could curl up against his and he could stroke her hair and they could talk about their days and kiss and laugh without giving a flying rat's ass what anyone else saw, much less thought.

"Chadwick came by the office today."

It was a hard thing to watch, her reaction. She sat up, pulling away from his touch. Her shoulders straightened and her eyes took on a hard look. "Did he now?"

Ethan let his hand fall away. "He did."

She considered this new development for a moment. "I suppose Phillip talked to him?"

"I got that feeling. He also said I'm making him look bad, with all the flowers."

Frances waved this excuse away as if it were nothing more than a gnat. "He can afford to buy Serena flowers—and does, frequently." Her eyes closed and, elbows back on the table, she clasped her hands in front of her. She looked as though she was concentrating very hard—or praying. "Do I even want to know what he said?"

"The usual older-brother stuff. What are my intentions, I'd better not break his little sister's heart—that sort of thing." He shrugged, as if it'd been just another day at the office.

She opened her eyes and stared at him over the tops of her hands. "What did you say? Please tell me you didn't kowtow to him. It's not good for his already-massive ego."

Ethan leaned back. "I merely informed him that what happens between two consenting adults is none of his business and for him to presume he knows best for either of us was patronizing at best. A fact I have recently been reminded of myself."

Frances's mouth opened, but then what he said registered and she closed it again. A wry smile curved her lips. He wanted to kiss that smile, those lips—but there was a table in the way. "You didn't."

"I did. I don't recall any kowtowing."

She laughed at that, which made him feel good. It wasn't as if he'd fought to the death for her honor or anything, but he'd still protected her from a repeat of what had happened last night.

She shifted and the toes of her foot came into contact with his shin. Slowly, she stroked up and down. His pulse kicked it up another notch—then two.

"I got you something," he said suddenly. He had decided it would be better to wait to give her the jewelry until after dinner, but the way she was looking at him? The way she was touching him? He'd changed his mind.

"The flowers were beautiful," she murmured. Her foot moved up and then down again, stroking his desire higher.

The room was too warm. Too hot. He was going to fall into the flames and get burned, and he couldn't think of a better way to go.

He reached into his pocket and pulled out the long, thin

velvet box. "I picked it out," he told her, holding it out to her. "I thought it suited you."

Her foot paused against his leg, and he took advantage of the break to adjust his pants. Sitting had suddenly become uncomfortable.

Her eyes were wide as she stared at the box. "What did you do?"

"I bought my future wife a gift," he said simply. The words felt right on his tongue, like they belonged there. *Wife*. "Open it."

She hesitated, as if the box might bite her. So he opened it for her.

The diamond necklace caught the light and glittered. He'd chosen the drop pendant, a square-cut diamond that hung off the end of a chain of three smaller diamonds, all set in platinum. Tiffany's had some larger solitaires, but this one seemed to fit Frances better.

"Oh, Ethan," she gasped as he held the box out toward her. "I didn't expect this."

"I like to keep you guessing," he told her. He set the box down and pulled the platinum chain out of its moorings. "Here," he said, his voice deeper than he remembered it being. "Allow me."

He stood and moved behind her, draping the necklace in front of her. She swept her mane of hair away from her neck, exposing the smooth skin. Ethan froze. He wanted nothing more than to lean down and taste her, to run his lips over the delicate curve where her neck met her shoulders—to see how she would react if he trailed kisses lower, pulling the dress down farther until...

She tilted her head down, pulling him back to the reality of standing in a crowded restaurant, holding nine thousand dollars' worth of diamonds. As he tried to fasten the clasp, his hands began to shake with need—the need to hold her, the need to stroke her bare shoulders. The need to make her *his*.

He'd had other lady friends, bought them nice gifts—usually when it was time for him to move on—but he had never felt this much need before. He didn't know what it was—only that it was because of her.

He willed his hands—and other body parts—to stand down. This was just a temporary madness; that was all. A beautiful woman in a gorgeous dress designed to inspire lust—nothing more, really.

Except it wasn't. No matter what he told himself, he knew he wasn't being honest—not with himself, not with her.

Honesty was not supposed to figure into this, after all. The whole premise of their relationship was based on a stack of lies that only got taller with each passing day and each passing floral arrangement. No, it was not supposed to be honest, their relationship. It was, however, supposed to be simple. She needed the money. He needed the Beaumont seal of approval. Everyone came out a winner.

That was possibly the biggest lie of all. Nothing about Frances Beaumont had been simple since the moment he'd laid eyes on her.

Finally, he got the clasp hooked. He managed to restrain himself enough that he did not press a kiss to her neck, did not wind her long hair into his hands.

But he was not exactly restrained. His fingertips drifted over the skin she'd exposed when she'd moved her hair and then down her bare shoulders with the lightest of touches. It shouldn't have been overtly sexual, shouldn't have been all that erotic—but unfamiliar need hammered through his gut.

It only got worse when she let go of her hair and that mass of fire-red silk brushed over the backs of his hands. Without meaning to—without meaning any of this—he dug his fingers into her skin, pulling her against him. She was soft and warm, and she leaned back and looked up at him.

Their gazes met. He supposed that, with another woman, he'd be staring down her front, looking at how his diamonds were nestled between her breasts, so large and firm and on such display at this angle.

But he was only dimly aware of her cleavage because Frances was staring up at him, her lips parted ever so slightly. Color had risen in her cheeks, and her eyes were wide. One of her hands reached up and found his. It was only when she pressed his hand flat against her skin that he realized his palms were moving along her skin, moving to feel everything about her—to learn everything about her.

He stroked his other thumb over her cheek. She gasped, a small movement that he felt more than saw. His body responded to her involuntary reaction with its own. Blood pounded in his ears as it raced from his brain to his erection as fast as it could. And, given how she was leaning against it, she knew it, too.

This was the moment, he thought dimly—as much as he could think, anyway. She could say something cutting and put him in his place, and he'd have to sit down and eat dinner with blue balls and not touch her like he meant it.

"Ethan," she whispered as she stared up at him. Her eyes seemed darker now, the pupils widening until the blue-green had almost disappeared.

Yes, he wanted to shout, to groan—yes, yes. He wanted to hear his name on her lips, over and over, in the most intimate of whispers and the loudest of passionate shouts. He wanted to push her to the point where all she could do, say—think—was his name. Was him.

His hand slipped lower, stroking the exposed skin of her throat. Lower still, tracing the outline of the necklace he'd bought for her.

Her grip on his hand tightened as his fingers traced the pendant. She didn't tell him to stop, though. She didn't lean away, didn't give a single signal that he should stop touching her. His hand started to move even lower, stroking down into the body of her dress and—

"Are we ready to order?" a too-bright, too-loud voice suddenly demanded.

Frances and Ethan both jumped. Suddenly he was aware that they were still in public, that at least half the restaurant was still watching them—that he'd been on the verge of sheer insanity in the full view of anyone with a cell phone. What the hell was wrong with him?

He tried to step away from her, to put at least a respectable three inches between their bodies—but Frances didn't let go of his hand.

Instead—incredibly—she stood and said, "Actually, I'm not hungry. Thanks, though." Then she turned to give him a look over her shoulder. "Shall we?"

"We shall," was the most intelligent thing he was capable of coming up with. The waiter smirked at them both as Ethan fished a fifty out of his wallet to cover his bar tab.

Every eye was on them as they swept up to the front together. Ethan took Frances's coat from the coat check girl and held it as Frances slipped her bare arms into it. They didn't speak as they braved the cold wind and waited for the valet to bring his car around. But Ethan put his arm around her shoulders and pulled her close. She leaned her head against his chest. Was he imagining things, or was she breathing hard—or at least, harder than normal? He wasn't sure. Maybe that was his chest, rising and falling faster than he normally breathed.

He didn't feel normal. Sex was always fun, always enjoyable—but something he could take or leave. He liked the release of it, and, yeah, sometimes he needed that release more than other times. But that's all it was. A pressure valve that sometimes needed to be depressurized a bit.

It wasn't this pain that made thinking rationally impossible—a pain that could only be erased by burying himself in her body over and over again until he was finally sated.

This wasn't about a simple release. He could achieve that with anyone. Hell, he didn't even need another person.

But this? Right now? This was about Frances and this unknown need she inspired in him. And the more he tried to name that need, the more muddled his head became. He wanted to show her what he could do for her, how he could take care of her, protect her and honor her. That they could be good together. For each other.

Finally, the car arrived. Ethan held her door for her and then got behind the wheel. He gunned it harder than he needed to, but he didn't want to waste another minute, another second, without Frances in his arms.

They weren't far from the hotel. He wouldn't have even bothered with the car if it'd been twenty degrees warmer. The drive would take five minutes, tops.

Or it would have—until Frances leaned over and placed her hand on his throbbing erection. Even through the layers of his boxers and wool trousers, her touch burned hot as she tested his length. Ethan couldn't do anything but grip the steering wheel as she made her preliminary exploration of his arousal.

It was when she squeezed him, shooting the pain that veered into pleasure through his whole body, that he forced out the words. "This isn't a game, Frances."

"No, it's not," she agreed, her voice breathy as her fingers stroked him. His body burned for her. If she stopped, he didn't know if he could take it. "Not anymore."

"Are you coming up to my room?" It came out far gruffer than he'd intended—not a request but not quite a demand.

"I don't think the hotel staff would appreciate it if we had sex in the lobby." She didn't let go of him when she said it. If anything, her hand was tighter around him.

"Is that what you really want? Sex, I mean. Not the lobby part." Because he was honor-bound to ask and more than honor-bound to accept her answer as the final word on the matter. Even if it killed him. "Because it wasn't part of the original deal."

That pushed her away from him. Her hot hand was gone, and he was left aching without her touch. "Ethan," she said in the most severe voice he'd heard her use all night long. "I don't want to talk about the damned deal. I don't want to think about it."

"Then what do you want?" he asked as they pulled up in front of the hotel.

She didn't answer. Instead, she got out, and he had no choice but to follow her, handing his keys to the valet. They walked into the hotel without touching, waited for the elevator without speaking. Ethan was thankful his coat was long enough to hide his erection.

They walked into the elevator together. Ethan waited until the doors were closed before he moved on her. "Tell me what you want, Frances," he said, pinning her against the back of the elevator. Her body was warm against his as she looked up at him through her lashes and he saw her. Not her armor, not her carefully constructed front— he saw *her*. "To hell with the deal. Tell me what you want right now. Is it sex? Is it *me*?"

"I shouldn't want you," she said, her voice soft, almost uncertain. She took his face in her hands, their mouths a whisper away. "I shouldn't."

"I shouldn't want you, either," he told her, an unfamiliar flash of anger pushing the words out of his mouth. "You drive me mad, Frances. Absolutely freaking mad. You undermine me at the Brewery and work me into a lather, and you turn my head around so fast that I get dizzy every time I see you. And, damn it all, you do it with that smile that lets me know it's easy for you. That *I'm* easy for you." He touched his thumb to her lips. She tried to kiss his thumb, and when he pulled it away, she tried to kiss him, pulling his head down to hers.

He didn't let her. He peeled her hands off his face and pinned them against the elevator walls. For some reason, he had to tell her this now before they went any further. "You *complicate* things. God help me—you make everything harder than it has to be, and I don't want you any other way."

Her eyes were wide, although he didn't know if that was because he was holding her captive or what he'd said. "You…don't?"

"No, I don't. I want you complicated and messy." He leaned against her, so she could feel exactly how much he wanted her. "I want you taunting and teasing me, and I want you with your armor up because you're the toughest woman I know. And I want you with your armor off entirely because—" Abruptly, the flash of anger that gave him all of those words was gone, and he realized that instead of telling a beautiful woman how wonderful she was, he was pretty sure he'd been telling her that she irritated him. "Because that's how I want you," he finished, unsure of himself.

Her lips parted and her mouth opened—right as the elevator did the same. They were on Ethan's floor. He held her like that for just a second longer, then released his hold in time to keep the doors from closing on them.

He held out his hand for her.

And he waited.

Twelve

"You *want* me complicated?" Frances stood there, staring at Ethan as if he'd casually announced he wore a cape in his off time while fighting crime.

No one had wanted her messy and complicated before. They wanted her simply, as an object of lust or as a step up the social ladder. It was when things got messy or complicated or—God help her—both that men disappeared from her life. When Frances dared to let her real self show through—that was when the trouble began. She was too dramatic, too high-maintenance, her tastes and ambitions too expensive. Her family life was far too complex—that was always rich, coming from the ones who wanted an association with the prestige of the Beaumont name but none of the actual work that went into maintaining it.

She'd heard it all before. *So* many times before.

The elevator beeped in warning. Ethan said, "I do," and grabbed her, hauling her past the closing doors.

She didn't know what to say to that, which was a rarity in itself. They stood in the middle of the hallway for a moment, Ethan holding on to her hand tightly. "Do you?" he asked in a gentle voice. "Want me, that is."

She felt the cool weight of the diamonds he'd laid against her skin. How many thousands of dollars had he spent on them? On her? It was not supposed to be complicated. If they had sex, then it was supposed to be this simple quid pro quo. This was the way of her world—it always had been. The man buys an expensive, extravagant gift and the woman takes her clothes off. It was not messy.

Except it was.

"You're ruining the last of my family's legacy and business," she told him. "You're everything that went wrong. When we lost the Brewery, I lost a part of my identity and I should hate you for being party to that. God, how I wanted to hate you."

Oh, Lord—were her eyes watering? No. Absolutely not. There was no crying in baseball or in affairs of the heart. At least, not in her affairs of the heart, mostly because her affairs never actually involved her heart.

She kept that locked away from everyone, and no one had ever realized it—until Ethan Logan had shown up and seen the truth of the matter. Until he'd seen the truth of her.

"You can still hate me in the morning," he told her. "I don't expect anything less from you."

"But what about tonight?" Because it was all very well and good to say that he liked her messy, but that didn't mean she wasn't still a mess. And that wore on a man after a while.

He stepped into her. His body was strong and warm, and she knew if she gave first and leaned against him, breathed in his woodsy scent, that she would be lost to him.

She'd already lost so much. Could she afford to lose anything else?

He stroked his fingers down her face, then slid them back through her hair, pulling her up to him. "Let me love you tonight, Frances. Just you and me. Nothing else."

It was real and honest and sincere, damn him to hell. It was true because he was true. None of those little lies and half glosses of compliments that hid the facts better than they illuminated them. And for a man who did not grasp the finer points of sweet nothings, it was the sweet-est damn something she'd ever heard.

A door behind them opened. She didn't know if it was the elevator or another guest and she didn't much care. She took off down the hall toward Ethan's room without letting go of his hand.

He got the door open and pulled her inside. "I won't like you in the morning," she told him, her voice shaking as he undid the belt at her waist and pushed the coat from her shoulders.

"But you like me now," he replied, shucking his own coat in the process. "Don't you?"

She did. Oh, this was a heartache waiting to happen, this thing between her and Ethan.

"I don't want to talk anymore," she said in as command-ing a voice as she could muster. More than that, she didn't want to think anymore. She only wanted to feel, to get lost in the sweet freedom of surrendering to her baser lust.

She grabbed him by the suit jacket and jerked it down his arms, trying to get him as naked as possible as fast as possible. He let her, but he said, "Don't you dare hide be-hind that wall, Frances."

"I'm not hiding," she informed him, grabbing his belt and undoing it. "I'm getting you naked. That's generally how sex works best."

The next thing she knew, they were right back to where they'd been in the elevator, with the full weight of his body pinning her against the door, her wrists in his hands. "Don't," he growled at her. "I don't want to sleep with your armor. I want to sleep with you, damn it. I *like* you. Just the way you are. So don't try to be some flippant, distant princess who's above this. Above us."

Her breath caught in her throat. "You don't know what you're asking of me." It didn't come out confident or cocky or even flippant.

"Maybe I do." He kissed her then, with enough force to knock her head back. "Sorry," he murmured against her lips.

"It's okay," she replied because if they were getting to the sex part, they'd stop talking and she could just feel. Even the small pain in the back of her head was okay because she didn't have to talk about it, about what it really meant. "Just keep kissing me hard."

"Is that how you want it?"

She tested her wrists against his grip. There was a little give, but not much. "Yes," she said, knowing full well that he was a man who knew exactly what that meant. "That's how I want *you*." Hard and fast with no room to stop and think. None.

A deep sound came out of his chest, a growl that she felt in her bones. His hips shifted and his erection ground against her. Yes, she wanted to feel all of that.

But then he said, "Tell me if something doesn't work," and she heard his control starting to fray. "Promise me that, babe."

She blinked up at him through a haze of desire. Had anyone ever said that to her before? "Of course," she said, trying to make it sound as though all of her previous lovers had put her orgasms first—had put her first.

He raised an eyebrow at her. He didn't even have to say it—she could still hear him telling her not to pretend.

Then he moved. "Whatever else," he said as he slid her hands up over her head and put both her wrists under one of his massive hands, "I expect complete and total honesty in bed."

"We aren't currently in bed," she reminded him. She tested her wrists again, but he wasn't playing around. He had her pinned.

It wasn't that she wasn't turned on—she was. But a new kind of excitement started to build underneath the standard sexual arousal that she normally felt. Ethan had her pinned. He had a free hand. He could do anything that he wanted to her.

And he'd stop the moment she told him to.

For once in her life, she wouldn't have to think about anything except what he was going to do next.

"Turn around," he ordered as he lifted her wrists away from the door just enough that she could spin in place. Then he swept her hair away from her neck and—and—oh, God. He didn't just kiss her there, he scraped his teeth over her exposed skin, raw and hungry.

Frances sucked in air at the unexpected sensation. "Good?" he asked.

"Yeah."

"Good," he said, biting a little harder this time, then kissing the sore spot.

Frances shifted, the weight between her legs growing hotter and heavier as he worked over her skin. Then he was pulling the zipper down on her dress, and the whole thing fell to her feet, leaving her in nothing but a white lace pair of panties that left very little to the imagination.

"Oh, babe," Ethan said in undisguised appreciation. She started to turn so she could see his face when he said it, but he gave her bottom a light smack and then used his body to keep hers flat against the door. "No, don't look," he ordered. "Just feel."

"Yeah," she moaned, her skin slightly stinging from where he'd smacked her. "I want to feel you."

His hand popped against her bare bottom again—not hard. He wasn't hurting her. But the unexpected contact made her body involuntarily tighten, and the anticipation of the next touch drove everything else from her mind.

Ethan's free hand circled her waist, pushing her just far enough away from the door that he could cup one of her breasts, teasing the nipple until it was hard with desire.

Then he tugged at it with more force. "Yeah?" he asked, his breath hot against her neck. He shoved one of his knees between her legs and she sagged onto it, grinding her hips, trying to take the pressure off the one spot in her body that made standing hard.

"Yeah," she moaned, her body moving without her permission, trying to find release, that moment where there was a climax that only Ethan could bring her to.

"You want more?" he demanded, tugging at her nipple again.

"Ethan, please," she panted, for no matter how she shifted her hips, the only pressure she felt did not push her over the edge.

He pulled away from her. "Don't move," he said. Then her wrists were free and his knee was gone and she felt cold, pressed up against this impersonal hotel door. Behind her, she heard the sound of plastic tearing. The condom. *Good.*

Then Ethan put his hand on the back of her neck and pulled her away from the door. "Hard?" he asked again, as if he wanted to make absolutely sure.

"Hard," she all but begged. "Hard and fast and—"

He led her to the bed, but instead of laying her out on it, he bent her over the edge. Her panties were pulled down, and she was exposed before him.

Her body quivered with need and anticipation and excitement because this was not gentle and sweet, not when he grabbed her by the hips and lifted her bottom against his rock-hard erection. His fingers dug into her flesh in a hungry way.

"Ethan," she moaned as he smacked her bottom again, just hard enough that her muscles tightened and she almost came right then. She fisted the bedclothes in her hands and tensed, hoping and praying for the next touch. "Hard and fast and now. Now, Ethan, or I won't like you in the morning, I swear to God, I'll hate you. *Now*, Ethan, *now*."

Then he was against her, and, with a moan of pure masculine satisfaction, he was in her, thrusting hard. Frances gasped at the suddenness of him—oh, he was huge—but her body took him in as he pounded her with all the aggression she needed so badly.

She hit her peak, moaning into the sheets as the wave cascaded over her. *Thank heavens*, she thought, going soft after it'd passed. She'd wanted to come so badly and—and—

And Ethan didn't stop. He didn't sputter to a finish. Instead, he paused long enough to reach forward and tangle his hands in her hair and pull so that her head came off the bed. "Are you nice and warmed up now?" he demanded, and a shiver ran through her body. He felt it, too—she could tell by the way he twined her hair around her fingers. "That's it, babe. Ready?"

He wasn't done. Oh, he wasn't done with her. He was going to make her come again, so fast and so hard that when he began to thrust again, all she could do was take him in. He kept one hand tangled in her hair, lifting her head up and back so that she arched away from him and her bottom lifted up to his greedy demands.

All she could do was moan—she wanted to cry out, but the angle of her neck made that too hard. Everything about her tightened as Ethan gave her exactly what she wanted—him, hard and fast.

This time, when he brought his hand against her ass in time with his thrusting, she came equally as hard. She couldn't help it. Her body acted without her input at all. All she was, all she could feel, was what Ethan did to her. The climax was unlike anything she'd ever felt before, so intense she forgot to breathe even.

Ethan held her there as waves of pleasure washed her

clean of everything but satisfaction. When she sagged against the bed, spent and panting, he let go of her hair, dug his fingertips back into her hips and pumped into her three more times before groaning and falling forward onto her.

They lay there for a moment, his body pressing hers against the mattress while she tried to remember how to breathe like a normal human. She didn't feel normal anymore; that was for sure.

She didn't know how she felt. Good—oh, yes. She felt wonderful. Her body was limp and her skin tingled and everything was amazing.

But when Ethan rolled off her and then leaned down and pressed a kiss between her shoulder blades—she felt decidedly not normal. She didn't turn her head to look at him. She didn't know what to say. Her! Frances Beaumont! Speechless! That was hard enough to accomplish by itself—but to have had sex so intense and so satisfying that she had not a single snappy observation or cutting comeback?

Not that he was waiting for her to say something. He kissed her on the shoulder and said, "I'll be right back," before he hefted himself off the bed. She heard the bathroom door click shut, and then she was alone in the hotel room with only her feelings.

Now what was she going to do?

Thirteen

Ethan splashed cold water on his face, trying to get his head to clear. He felt like a jackass. That wasn't how he normally took a woman to bed. Not even close. He usually took his time, making sure the foreplay left everyone satisfied before the actual sex.

But pinning Frances against the door and then bending her over the edge of the bed? Pawing at her as if he were little more than a lust-crazed animal? That hadn't been tender and sweet.

He didn't want to be responsible for his actions. He'd smacked her bottom—more than once! That wasn't like him. He wanted that to be her fault—she'd worn the red dress, she'd been this *siren* that pushed him past sanity, past responsibility.

But that was crap, and he knew it. All she'd said was that she wanted it hard and fast. He could have still been a gentleman about it. Instead, he'd gotten rough. He'd never done that before. He didn't know...

Well, he just didn't know.

And he wasn't going to find out hiding in the bathroom.

He'd apologize; that was all there was to it. He'd gotten carried away. It wouldn't happen again.

He finished up and headed out. He hadn't even gotten undressed. He'd stripped her down, but aside from shoving his pants out of the way, he was still dressed. Yes, that was quite possibly the best sex of his life, but still. He couldn't shake the feeling that he'd gone too far.

That feeling got even stronger when he saw her. Frances had curled up on her side. She looked impossibly small against the expanse of white sheets. She watched him, her eyes wide. Was she upset? *Hell.*

Then her nose wrinkled, and he was pretty sure she smiled. "You're not naked," she said. Her voice was raw, as if she'd been shouting into the wind for hours.

"Is that a problem?" He tried to keep it casual sounding. He wasn't sure he made it.

She uncurled from the bed like a flower opening for him. "I wanted to see you. And I didn't get to."

"My apologies for the disappointment." He started to jerk open the buttons on his shirt, but she stood and closed the distance between them. His hands fell around her waist, still warm from the sex. He wanted to fold her into his arms and hold her for as long as he could.

Where was all this ridiculous sentiment coming from? He wasn't a sentimental guy.

"Let me," she said. He saw that her hands were trembling. "And it wasn't disappointing. It was wonderful. Except that I couldn't see you."

Ethan blinked twice, trying to process that. "I didn't go too far?"

"No," she said, giving him a nervous smile. "I—" She paused and took a deep breath. "Honestly?"

"Even though we're still not in bed," he said with a grin, tilting her chin up so he could look her in the eyes.

She held his gaze for a moment before forcibly turning her attention back to his buttons. "Thank you," she said quietly.

That was not quite what he'd been expecting. "For what? I think I got just as much out of that as you did."

She undid the last button and pushed the shirt off him. Then his T-shirt followed. Finally she shoved his pants down, and Ethan kicked out of them.

"Oh, my," she whispered, skimming her fingers over his chest and ruffling his hair.

He fought the urge to flex. The urge won. She giggled as his muscles moved under her hands. "Ethan!"

"Sorry," he said, walking her back toward the bed. "I can't seem to help myself around you."

This time, they actually got under the covers. Ethan pulled her on top of him. He didn't mean it in an explicitly sexual way, but her body covering his? Okay, it was more than a little sexual. "Why did you thank me?"

She laid out on him, her head tucked against his chest. "You really want me messy and complicated?"

"Seems to be working so far."

She sighed, tracing small circles against his skin. "No one's ever wanted me. Not the real me. Not like this."

"I find that hard to believe. You are a hell of a woman."

"They don't want me," she insisted. "They want the fantasy of me. Beautiful and sexy and rich and famous. They want the mystique of the Beaumont name. That's what I am to people." When he didn't have a response to that, she propped herself up on one elbow and stared down at him. "That's what I was to you, wasn't I?"

There was no point in playing games about it. "You were. But you're not anymore."

Her smile was tinged with sadness. "I'm not used to being honest, I guess."

He cupped her face in his hands and kissed her. He didn't intend for it to be a distraction, but she must have taken it that way because she pulled back. "Why did you agree to a sham marriage? And don't give me that line about the workers loving me."

"Even though they do," he put in.

"Most men do not agree to sham marriages as business deals," she went on as if he hadn't interrupted her. "I seem to recall you making quite a point of saying love wasn't a part of marriage when we came to terms. So spill it."

She had him trapped. Sure, he could throw her off him, but then she shifted and straddled him, and his body stirred at the thought of her bare legs wrapped around his waist, her body so close to his.

So, with mock exasperation, he flopped back against the bed. "My parents have an…unusual relationship," he said.

She leaned down on him, her arms crossed over her chest, her chin on her arms. "I don't want you to take this the wrong way, but so? I mean, my mom was second out of four wives for my dad. I wouldn't know a usual relationship if it bit me. Present company included."

He wrapped his arms around her body, enjoying the warmth she shared with him. No, this wasn't usual, not even close. But he was enjoying it anyway. "Have you ever heard of Troy Logan?"

"No. Brother or father?"

He wasn't surprised. Her brother Chadwick would probably recognize the name, but that wasn't Frances's world. "Father. Notorious on Wall Street for buying companies and dismantling them at a profit."

She tilted her head from side to side. "I take it the apple did not fall terribly far from the tree?"

"I don't take companies apart. I restructure them." She gave him an arch look, and he gave in. "But, yes, you're correct. We're in nearly the same line of work."

"And…" she said. "Your mother?"

"Wanda Kensington." He braced for the reaction.

He didn't have to wait long. She gasped, which made him wince. "What? You don't mean—*the* Wanda Kensington? The artist?"

"I can't tell you how rare it is that someone knows my

mother's name but not my father's," he said, stroking her hair away from her face.

"Don't change the subject," she snapped, sitting all the way up. Which left her bare breasts directly in Ethan's line of sight. The diamonds he'd bought for her glittered between those perfect breasts. "Your mother is—but Wanda's known for her art installations! Massive performance pieces that take like a year to assemble! I don't ever remember reading anything about her having a family."

"She wasn't around much. I don't know why they got married, and I don't know why they stayed married. I'm not even sure they like each other. They never made sense," he admitted. "She'd be gone for months, a year—we had nannies that my father was undoubtedly sleeping with—and then she'd walk back in like no time at all had passed and pretend to be this hands-on mother who cared."

He was surprised to hear the bitterness in his voice. He'd long ago made peace with his mother. Or so he'd thought. "And she'd try, I think. She'd stick it out for a few weeks—once she was home for almost three months. She made it to Christmas, and then she was gone again. We never knew, my brother and I. Never had a clue when she'd show up or when she'd disappear again."

"So you were—what? Another piece of performance art? The artist as a mother?"

"I suppose." Not that he'd ever thought about it in those terms. "It wasn't bad. Dad wasn't jealous of her. She wasn't jealous of him. It wasn't like there was drama. It was just... a marriage on paper."

"It was a sham," Frances corrected.

He skimmed his hands up and down her thighs, shifting her weight against him. His erection was more than interested in the shifting. "Didn't seem like it'd be hard to replicate," he agreed.

But that was before—before he'd seen past Frances's

armor, before he'd stupidly begun to like the real woman underneath.

She rocked her hips, and his body responded. He stroked her nipples—this time, without the roughness—and Frances moaned appreciatively. He shouldn't want her this much, shouldn't *like* her this much. Passion wasn't supposed to figure into his plans. It never had before.

He lifted her off long enough to roll on another condom, and then she settled her weight back onto him, taking him in with a sigh of pure pleasure. *This* was honesty. This was something real between them because she meant something more to him than just her last name.

She rode him slowly, taking her time, letting him play with her breasts and her nipples until she was panting and he was driving into her. He leaned forward enough to catch one of her breasts in his mouth and sucked her nipple hard between his teeth.

She might not like him in the morning, and she'd be well within her rights.

But he was going to like her. Hell, he already did. It was going to be a huge problem.

As she shuddered down on him, urging him to suck her nipples harder as she came apart, he didn't care. Complicated and messy and his.

She was his.

After she'd collapsed onto him and he'd taken care of the condom, they lay in each other's arms. He had things he wanted to say to her, except he didn't know what those things were, which wasn't like him. He was a decisive man. The buck stopped with him.

"Are we still going to get married next week?" she asked in a drowsy voice.

"If you want," he said, feeling even as he said it that it was not the best response. He tried again. "I thought we weren't going to talk about the deal tonight."

"We aren't," she agreed and then immediately qualified that statement. "It's just that…this changes things."

"Does it?" He leaned over and turned out the light and then pulled the covers up over them both. When was the last time he'd had a woman spend the night in his arms? He couldn't think of when. His previous relationships were not spend-the-night relationships.

He tucked his arm around her body and held her close. Something cold and metallic poked at his side—the necklace. It was all she had on.

"We were supposed to barely live together," she reminded him. "We weren't supposed to sleep together. We weren't…"

He yawned and shrugged. "So we'll be slightly more married than we planned on. The marital bed and all that."

"And you're okay with that?"

"I'm okay with you." He kissed the top of her head. "I guess… Well, when we made the deal, I didn't think I'd enjoy spending time with you."

"You mean sex. You didn't think you'd enjoy sleeping with me." She sounded hurt about that, although he couldn't tell if she was playing or actually pouting.

"No, I don't," he clarified. "I mean, I didn't think I'd want to spend time with you. I didn't think I'd like you this much."

The moment the words left his mouth, he knew that he'd said too much. Damn it, they were supposed to roll over and go to sleep and not have deep, meaningful conversations until he'd recovered from the sex and had some more.

Instead, Frances tensed and then sat up, pulling away from him. "Ethan," she said, her voice a warning. "I told you not to like me."

"You make it sound like I have a choice about it," he said.

"You do."

"No, I don't. I can't help it." She didn't reply, didn't curl back into his arms. "We don't have to rush to get married. I'm willing to wait for you."

"Jesus," she said. The bed shifted, and then she was out of it, fumbling around the room in the dark. "Jesus, you sound like you *want* to marry me."

He turned on the light. "What's wrong?"

She threw his words back at him. "What's wrong?" She grabbed her dress and started to shimmy into it. Any other time, watching Frances Beaumont get dressed would be the highlight of his day. But not now, not when she was angrily trying to jerk up the zipper.

"Frances," he said, getting out of bed. "Where are you going?"

"This was a mistake," was the short reply.

He could see her zipping into her armor as fast as the dress—if not faster. "No, it wasn't," he said defensively, trying to catch her in his arms. "This was good. Great. This was us together. This is what we could be."

"Honestly, Ethan? There is no us. Not now, not ever. My God," she said, pushing him away and snagging her coat. "I thought you were smarter than this. Good sex and you're suddenly in love—in like?" she quickly corrected. "Unacceptable."

"Like hell it is," he roared at her.

"This is causal at best, Ethan. *Casual.* Casual sex, casual marriage." She flung her coat over her barely zipped dress and hastily knotted the belt. "I warned you, but you didn't listen, did you?"

"Would you calm the hell down and tell me what's wrong?" he demanded. "I did listen. I listened when you told me you expected to be courted with flowers and gifts and thoughtfulness."

"I did not—"

But he cut her off. "I listened when you told me about

your plans for a gallery. I listened when your family caught you off guard."

"I do not like you." She bit the words off as if she were killing them, one syllable at a time.

"I don't believe you. Not anymore. I've seen the real you, damn it all."

She drew herself up to her full height, a look on her face like a reigning monarch about to deliver a death sentence. "Have you?" she said. "I thought you were better at the game than this, Ethan. How disappointing that you're like all the rest."

And then she was gone. The door to the room swung open and slammed shut behind her, leaving Ethan wondering what the holy hell had just happened.

Fourteen

When had Frances lost control? That was the question she kept asking herself on the insanely long elevator ride down to the hotel lobby. She asked it as the valet secured a cab for her, and she asked it again on the long ride out to the mansion.

Because she had. She'd lost all sorts of control.

She slipped into the mansion. The place was dark and quiet—but then, it was late. Past midnight. The staff had left hours ago. Chadwick and Serena and their little girl were no doubt asleep, as were Frances's younger siblings.

She felt very much alone.

She took off her shoes and tiptoed up to her room. She jerked her zipper down so hard she heard tearing, which was a crying shame because this dress was her best one. But she couldn't quite care.

Frances dug out her ugly flannel pajamas, bright turquoise plaid and baggy shapelessness. They were warm and soft and comforting, and far removed from the nothing she'd almost fallen asleep wearing when she'd been in bed with Ethan.

God, what a mess. And, yes, she was aware that she was probably making it messier than it had to be, just by virtue of being herself.

But was he serious? Sure, she could have believed it if

he'd said he loved being with her and she was special and wonderful before the sex. It was expected, those words of seduction. Except he hadn't said them then. He'd said things that should have been insults—that she made his life harder than he wanted her to, that she drove him mad, that she was a complicated hot mess.

Those were not the words of a man trying to get laid.

Those were the words of an honest man.

And then after? To lay there in his arms and feel as if she'd exposed so much more than her body to him and to have him tell her that he enjoyed being with her, that he liked her, that—

That he'd happily push back their agreed-on marriage because she was worth waiting for?

It was all supposed to be a game. A game she'd played before and a game she'd play again. Yes, this was the long game—a wedding, a yearlong marriage—but that didn't change the rules.

Did it?

She climbed under her own covers in her own bed, a bed that was just as large as Ethan's. It felt empty compared with what she'd left behind.

Ethan wasn't following the rules. He was changing them. She'd warned him against doing so, but he was doing so anyway. And it was all too much for Frances. Too much honesty, too much realness. Too much intimacy.

Men had proposed before. Professed their undying love and admiration for her. But no one had ever meant it. No one ever did, not in her world. Love was a bargaining chip, nothing more. Sex was calling a bluff. All a game. Just a game. If you played it right, you got diamonds and houses and money. And if you lost…you got nothing.

Nothing.

She curled up into a tight ball, just like she'd always done back when she was little and her parents were fighting. On bad nights, she'd sneak into Byron's room and curl up in his bed. He took the top half and she took the bottom, their backs touching. That's how they'd come into this world. It felt safer that way.

Once, Mom had loved Dad. And Dad must have had feelings for Mom, right? That's why he'd married her and made their illegitimate child, Matthew, legitimate.

But they couldn't live together. They couldn't share a roof. They'd have been better off like Ethan's folks, going their separate ways 85 percent of the time and only coming together when the stars aligned just so. And in the end, her father had won and her mother had lost, and that had been the game.

She almost got up and got her phone to call Byron. To tell him she might have been rash and that she needed to come hang out for a couple of days until things cooled off. Mom was out there, anyway.

It was late. Byron was probably still asleep.

And then there was Friday. Donut Friday.

She had to face Ethan again. With an audience. Just like they'd planned it.

She had nothing to wear.

Delores walked in with a stack of interoffice envelopes. Ethan glared at her, trying to get his heart to calm down.

He hadn't heard from Frances since she'd stormed out of his room two nights ago, and it was making him jumpy. He did not like being jumpy.

"Any donuts yet?" he made himself say casually.

"Haven't seen her yet, but I can check with Larry to find out if she's on the premises," Delores said in a genial manner. She handed him a rather thick envelope. It had no return address. It just said, "E. Logan."

"What's this?"

"I'm sure I don't know." When Ethan glared at her, she said, "I'll go check on those donuts."

The old battle-ax, he thought menacingly as he undid the clasp and slid out a half-inch-thick manila folder.

"Potentially of our mutual interest—C. Beaumont," proclaimed a small, otherwise benign yellow sticky note on the front of the folder.

The only feeling that Ethan did not enjoy more than jumpiness was uncertainty. And that's what the manila folder suddenly represented. What on earth would Chadwick Beaumont consider of mutual interest? The only thing that came to mind was Frances.

And what of Frances could merit a folder this thick?

The possibilities—everything from blackmail to depravities—ran together in his mind. He shoved them aside and opened the file.

And found himself staring at a dossier for one Zeb Richards, owner of ZOLA.

Ethan blinked in astonishment as he scanned the information. Zeb Richards, born in Denver in 1973, graduated from Morehouse College with a bachelor of arts degree and from the University of Georgia with a master's in business administration. Currently resided in New York. There was a small color photo of the man, the first that Ethan had seen.

Wait—had he met Zeb Richards before? There was something about the set of the man's jaw that looked familiar. He had dark hair that was cropped incredibly close to his head, the way many black men wore it.

But Ethan would remember meeting someone named Zeb, wouldn't he?

Then he flipped the page and found another document—a photocopy of a birth certificate. Well, he had to hand it to Chadwick—he was nothing if not thorough. The certificate confirmed that Zebadiah Richards was born in Denver in 1973. His mother was Emily Richards and his father was…

Oh, hell.

Under "Father" was the unmistakable name of one Hardwick James Beaumont.

Ethan flipped back to the photo. Yes, that jaw—that was like Chadwick's jaw, like Phillip's. Those two men had been unmistakably brothers—full brothers. The resemblance had been obvious. And they'd looked a fair deal like Frances. The jaw was softer on her, more feminine—more beautiful.

But if Zeb's mother had been African-American… That would account for everything else.

Oh, hell.

Suddenly, it all made sense. This agitation on behalf of ZOLA to sell the Beaumont Brewery? It wasn't a rival firm looking to discredit Ethan's company, and it wasn't an activist shareholder looking to peel the Beaumont Brewery off so it could pick it up for pennies on the dollar and sell it off, like Ethan's father did.

This was personal.

And it had nothing to do with Ethan.

Except he was, as of about two nights ago, sleeping with a Beaumont. He was probably still informally engaged to be married to said Beaumont, although he wouldn't be sure of that until the donut situation was confirmed. And, perhaps most important of all, he was currently running the Beaumont Brewery.

"Delores," he said into the intercom. "Was this envelope hand-delivered to you?"

"It was on my desk this morning, Mr. Logan."

"I need to speak to Chadwick Beaumont. Can you get me his number?"

"Of course." Ethan started to turn the intercom off, but then she added, "Oh, Ms. Beaumont is on the premises."

"Thank you," he said. He flipped the intercom off and stuffed the folder back into the envelope. It was no joke to say he was out of his league here. A bastard son coming back to wreak havoc on his half siblings? Yeah, Ethan was *way* out of his league.

Chadwick must have a sense of humor, what with that note about Zeb Richards being "potentially" a mutual interest.

But Frances—she didn't know anything about her siblings from unmarried mothers, did she? No, Ethan was certain he remembered her saying she didn't know any of them. Just that there were some.

So Zeb Richards was not, at this exact moment, something she needed to know about.

Unless…

He thought back to the way she'd stood before him last night, all of her armor fully in place while he'd been naked in every sense of the word. And she'd said—*No, be honest*, he told himself—*sneered* that she'd thought he'd be better at the game.

Was Zeb Richards part of the game?

Just because Frances said she didn't know any of the illegitimate Beaumonts didn't mean she'd been truthful about it.

She'd asked Ethan why he wanted to marry her. Had he asked why she'd agreed to marry him? Beyond the money for her art gallery?

What else was she getting out of their deal?

Why had she shown up with donuts last week?

The answer was right in front of him, a manila folder in an envelope.

Revenge.

Hadn't she told him that she'd lost part of herself when the family lost the Brewery? And hadn't she said she should hate him for his part in that loss?

What had seemed like a distant coincidence—Frances disrupting his personal life at nearly the exact same time some random investor was trying to disrupt his business—now seemed less like a coincidence and more like directly correlated events.

What if she not only knew Zeb Richards was her half brother—what if she was helping him? Getting insider information? Not from Ethan, necessarily—but from all the people here who loved and trusted her because she was their Frannie?

Did Chadwick know? Or did he suspect? Was that why he'd sent the file?

Ethan had assumed it'd been the encounter with Phillip Beaumont that had prompted Chadwick's appearance at the Brewery the other day. But what if there'd been something else? What if one of Chadwick's loyal employees had tipped him off that Frances was asking around, digging up dirt?

And if that was possible, who's side was Chadwick on? Ethan's? Frances's? Zeb Richards's?

Ethan's head began to ache. This, he realized with a half laugh, was what he was trying to marry into—a family so sprawling, so screwed up that they didn't even have a solid head count on all their relatives.

"She's here," Delores's voice interrupted his train of thought.

Ethan stood and straightened his tie. He didn't know why. He pushed the thought of bastards with an ax to grind out of his head. He had to focus on what was important here—Frances. The woman he'd taken to his bed last night and then promptly chased right out of it, all because he was stupid enough to develop feelings for her.

The woman who might be setting him up to fail because it was a game. Nothing but a game.

He had no idea which version of Frances Beaumont was on the other side of that door.

He wanted to be wrong. He wanted it to be one giant coincidence. He did not want to know that he'd misjudged her so badly, that he'd been played for such a fool.

Because if he had, he didn't know where he would go from here. He was still the CEO of this company. He still had a deal to marry her and invest in her gallery. He had his own company to protect. As soon as the Brewery was successfully restructured, he'd pull up stakes and move on to the next business that needed to be run with an iron fist and an eye to the bottom line. They'd divorce casually and go on with their lives.

And once he was gone, he'd never have to think about anything Beaumont ever again.

He opened his door. Frances was standing there in jeans and boots. She wore a thick, fuzzy cable-knit sweater, and her hair was pulled back into a modest bun. Not a sky-high heel or low-cut silk blouse in sight. She looked…plain, almost, which was something because if there was one thing Frances Beaumont wasn't, it was plain.

And despite the fact that his head felt as if an anvil had just been dropped on it, despite the fact that he was in over his head—despite the fact that, no, he was most likely not as good at the game as he'd thought he was and, no, she did not like him—he was glad to see her. He absolutely shouldn't be, but he was.

It only got worse when she lifted her head. There was no crowd today, no group of eager employees around to stroke her ego or destroy his. Just her and Delores and a box.

"Frances."

"Chocolate éclair?" she asked simply.

Even her makeup was simple today. She looked almost innocent, as if she was still trying to understand what had happened between them last night, just like he was.

But was that the truth of the matter? Or was this part of the game?

"I saved you two," she told him, holding the box out.

"Come in," he said, holding his door open for her. "Delores, hold my calls."

"Even—" she started to say.

"I'll call him back." Yes, he needed to talk to Chadwick, but he needed to talk to Frances more. He wasn't sleeping with Chadwick. Frances came first.

Frances paused, a look on her face that yesterday Ethan would have assumed to be confusion. Today? He couldn't be sure.

She walked past him, her head held high and her bearing regal. Ethan wanted to smile at her. Evening gowns or blue jeans, she could pull off imperial like nobody's business.

But he didn't smile. She did not like him. And liking her? Wanting to take care of her, to spend time with her? That had been a massive error on his part.

So the moment the door shut, he resolved that he would not care about her. He would not pull her into his arms and hold her tight and try to find the right sweet nothings to whisper in her ear to wipe that shell-shocked look off her face.

He would not comfort her. He couldn't afford to.

She carried the donut box over to the wagon-wheel coffee table and set it down. Then she sat on the love seat, tucking her feet up under her legs. "Hi," she said in what seemed like a small voice.

He didn't like it, that small voice, because it pulled at him, and he couldn't afford to let her play his emotions like that. "How are you today?" he asked politely. He went back to his desk and sat. It seemed like the safest place to be, with a good fifteen feet and a bunch of historic furniture between them.

She watched him with those big eyes of hers. "I brought you donuts," she said.

"Thank you." He realized his fingers were tapping on the envelope Chadwick had sent. He made them be still.

She said, "Oh. Okay," in such a disappointed voice that it almost broke him because he didn't want to disappoint her, damn it, and he was anyway.

But then, what was he supposed to do? He'd given her everything he had last night, and look how that had turned out. She'd cut him to shreds. She'd been disappointed that he'd liked her.

So she wasn't allowed to be disappointed that he was keeping his distance right now. End of discussion.

He stared at the envelope again. He had to know—how deep was she in this? "So," he said. "How are the plans for the art gallery going?"

"Fine. Are we…"

"Yes?"

She cleared her throat and stuck out her chin, as if she was trying to look tough and failing, miserably. "Are we still on? The deal, that is."

"Of course. Why would you think it's off?"

She took a deep breath. "I—well, I said some not-nice things last night. You've been nothing but wonderful and I… I was not gracious about it. About you."

Was she apologizing? For hurting his feelings? Not that he'd admit to having his feelings hurt.

Was it possible that, somewhere under the artifice, she actually cared for him, too?

No, probably not. This was just another test, another move. Ethan made a big show of shrugging. "At no point did I assume that this relationship—or whatever you want to call it—is based on 'niceness.'" She visibly winced. "You were right. Affection is irrelevant." This time, he did not offer to let her out of the deal or postpone the farce that would be their wedding. "And a deal's a deal, after all."

A shadow crossed her face, but only briefly. "Of course," she agreed. She wrapped her arms around her waist. She looked as though she was trying to hold herself together. "So we'll need to get engaged soon?"

"Tonight, if that's all right with you. I've made reservations for us as we continue our tour of the finer restaurants in Denver." He let his gaze flick over her outfit in what he hoped was judgment.

"Sounds good." That's what she said. But the way she said it? Anything but good.

"I did have a question," he said. "You asked me last night why I'd agreed to get married to you. To a stranger."

"Because it seems normal enough," she replied. He refused to be even the slightest bit pleased that she recalled their conversation about his parents. "And the workers love me."

He tilted his head in appreciation. "But when we were naked and sharing, I failed to ask what you were getting out of this deal. Why *you* would agree to marry a total stranger."

She paled, which made her red hair stand out that much more. "The gallery," she said in a shaky voice. "It's going to be my job, my space. Art is what I'm good at. I need the gallery."

"Oh, I'm quite sure," he agreed, swiveling his chair so he was facing her fully. His hand was tapping the envelope again. Damn that envelope. Damn Zebadiah Richards. Hell, while he was at it, damn Chadwick Beaumont, too. "But that's not all, is it?"

Slowly, her head moved from side to side, a no that she was apparently unaware she was saying. "Of course that's all. A simple deal."

"With the man who represented the loss of your family business and your family identity."

"Well, yes. That's why I need the gallery. I need a fresh start."

He leveled his stoniest glare at her, the one that produced results in business negotiations. The very look that usually had employees falling all over themselves to do what he wanted, the way he wanted it.

To her credit, she did not buckle. He would have been disappointed if she had, frankly. He watched her armor snap into place. But it didn't stop the rest of the color from draining out of her face.

He had her, and they both knew it.

"You wanted revenge."

The statement hung in the air. Frances's gaze darted from side to side as if she was looking for an escape route. When she didn't find what she wanted, she sat up straighter.

Good, Ethan thought. She was going to brazen this out. For some reason, he wanted it that way, wanted her to go down fighting. He didn't want her meek and apologetic and fragile, damn it. He wanted her biting and cutting, a warrior princess with words as weapons.

He wanted her messy and complicated, and, damn it all, he was going to get her that way. Even if it killed him.

"I don't know what you're talking about." As she said it, she uncurled on the couch. Her legs swung down and stretched out before her, long and lean, the very legs that had been wrapped around him. At the same time, she stretched up, thrusting out her breasts.

This time, he did smile. She was going to give him hell. *This* was the woman who'd walked into his office a week ago, using her body as a weapon of mass distraction.

This was the woman he could love.

He pushed that thought aside.

"How did you plan to do it?" he asked. "Did you plan on pumping me for information, or just gather some from the staff while you plied them with donuts?"

One eyebrow arched up. "*Plied?* Really, Ethan." She shifted forward, which would have worked much better to distract him if she'd been in a low-cut top instead of a sweater. "You make it sound like I was spiking the pastries with truth-telling serum."

He caught the glint of a necklace—his necklace, the one he'd given her last night. She was wearing it. For some reason, that distracted him far more than the seductive pose did.

"What I want to know," he said in a calm voice, "is if Richards contacted you first, or if you contacted him."

Her mouth had already opened to reply, but the mention of Richards's name pulled her up short. She blinked at him, her confusion obvious. Too obvious. "Who?"

"Don't play cute with me, Frances. You said so yourself, didn't you? This is all part of the game. I just didn't realize how far it went until this morning."

Her brow wrinkled. "I don't—who is Richards?"

"This innocent thing isn't working," he snapped.

Abruptly, she stood. "I don't know who Richards is. I didn't ply anyone with donuts to tell me anything they weren't willing to tell me anyway—which, for the most part, was how you were a jerk who didn't know the first thing about running the Brewery. So you can accuse me of plotting some unspecified revenge with some unspecified man named Richards, if that makes you feel better about not being able to do your own job without me smiling like an idiot by your side. But in the meantime, go to hell." She swept out of the room with all the cold grace he could have expected. She didn't even slam the door on the way out, probably because that would have been beneath her.

"Dinner tonight," he called after her, just so he could get in the last word.

"Ha!" he heard her say as she walked away from him.

Damn, that last bit had been more than loud enough that Delores would have heard. And Ethan knew that whatever Delores heard, the rest of the company heard.

The thing was, he was still no closer to an answer about Frances's level of involvement with ZOLA and Zeb Richards than he'd been before she'd shown up. He'd thought he'd learned how to read her, but last night, she'd made him question his emotional investment in her.

He had no idea how to trust anything she said or how to decide if she was telling the truth.

A phone rang. It sounded as if it came from a long way away. Delores stuck her head through the door. "I know you said to hold your calls," she said in a cautious voice, "but Chadwick's on the phone."

"I'll take it," he said because to pretend he was otherwise involved would look ridiculous.

He was going to get engaged tonight. Frances was supposed to start sleeping over. He was going to get married to her next weekend so he could maintain control over his company.

Because that was the deal.

He picked up his phone. "Who the hell is Zeb Richards?"

Fifteen

Frances found herself at the gallery—actually, at what would become the gallery. It wasn't a gallery yet. It was just an empty industrial space.

Becky was there with some contractors, discussing lighting options. "Oh, Frances—there you are," she said in a happy voice. But then she paused. "Are you okay?"

"Fine," Frances assured her. "Why would anything be wrong? Excuse me." She dodged contractors and headed back to the office. This room, at least, was suitable to hide in. It had walls, a door—and a lock.

Why would anything be wrong? She'd only screwed up. That wasn't unusual. That was practically par for the course. Ethan had been—well, he'd been wonderful. She'd spent a week with him. She'd let her guard down around him. She'd even slept with him—and he was amazing.

So of course she'd gone and opened her big mouth and insulted him, and now he was colder than a three-day-old fish.

She sat down at what would be her desk when she got moved in and stared at the bare wooden top. He'd said he liked her messy and complicated. And for a moment, she'd almost believed him.

But he hadn't meant it. Oh, he thought he had, of that she had no doubt. He'd thought he liked her all not simple.

He'd no doubt imagined he'd mastered the complexities of her extended family, besting her brothers in a show of sheer skill and Logan-based manliness.

The fool, she thought sadly. He'd gone and convinced himself that he could handle her. And he couldn't. Maybe no one could.

Then there'd been the conversation today. What the ever-loving hell had that been about? Revenge? Well, yeah—revenge had been part of it. She hadn't lied, had she? She'd told him that she'd lost part of herself when the Brewery had been sold. She just hadn't expected him to throw that back in her face.

And who the hell was this Richards she was supposed to be conspiring with?

Still, a deal was a deal. And as Ethan had made it quite clear that morning, it was nothing but a deal. She supposed she'd earned that.

It was better this way, she decided. She couldn't handle Ethan when he was being tender and sweet and saying absolutely ridiculous things like how he'd happily put the wedding off because she was worth the wait.

The sooner he figured out she wasn't worth nearly that much, the better.

The doorknob turned, but the lock held. This was followed by a soft knock. "Frances?" Becky said. "Can I come in?"

Against her better judgment, Frances got up and unlocked the door for her friend. A deal was a deal, after all—especially since Frances wasn't the only one who needed this gallery. Becky was depending on it just as much as Frances was. "Yes?"

Becky pushed her way into the office and shut the door behind her. "What's wrong?"

"Nothing," Frances lied. Too late, she remembered she

should try to look as if that statement were accurate. She attempted a lighthearted smile.

Becky's eyes widened in horror at this expression. "Ohmygosh—what happened?"

Maybe she wouldn't try to smile right now. It felt wrong, anyway. "Just a…disagreement. This doesn't change the deal. It's fine," Frances said with more force. "I just thought—well, I thought he was different. And I think he's really much the same."

That was the problem, wasn't it? For a short while, she'd believed Ethan might actually be interested in her, not her famous name or famous family.

Why hadn't she just taken him at his word? Why had she pushed and pushed and pushed, for God's sake, until whatever honest fondness he felt for her had been pushed aside under the glaring imperfection that was Frances Beaumont? Why couldn't she have just let good enough alone and accepted his flowers and his diamonds and his offers of affection and companionship?

Why did she have to ruin everything?

She'd warned him. She'd told him not to like her. She just hadn't realized that she'd do everything in her power to make sure he didn't.

She'd screwed up *so* much. She'd lost a fortune three separate times. Every endeavor she'd ever attempted outside of stringing a man along had failed miserably. She'd never had a relationship that could come close to breaking her heart because there was nothing to break.

So this relationship had been doomed from the get-go. Nothing lost, nothing gained. She was not going to let this gallery fail. She needed the steady job and the sense of purpose far more than she needed Ethan to look her in the eye and tell her that he wanted her just as complicated as she was.

Unexpectedly, Becky pulled her into a tight hug. "I'm so sorry, honey," she whispered into Frances's ear.

"Jeez, Becks—it was just a disappointing date. Not the end of the world." And the more Frances told herself that, the truer it'd become. "Now go," she said, doing her best to sound as if it was just another Friday at the office. "Contractors don't stand around for free."

She had to make this gallery work. She had to...

She had to do something to not think about Ethan.

That was going to be rather difficult when they had dinner tonight.

She wore the green dress. She felt more powerful in the green dress than she did in the bridesmaid's dress. And she'd only worn the green dress to the office, not out to dinner, so it wasn't like wearing the same outfit two days in a row.

The only person who would recognize the dress was Ethan, and, well, there was nothing to be done about that.

Frances twisted her hair up. The only jewelry she wore was the necklace. The one he'd gotten for her. It felt odd to wear it, to know he'd picked it out on his own and that, for at least a little while, she'd been swayed by something so cliché as diamonds.

But it was a beautiful piece, and it went with the dress. And, after all, she was getting engaged tonight so it only seemed right to wear the diamonds from her fiancé.

She swept into the restaurant, head up and smile firmly in place. She'd given herself a little pep talk about how this wasn't about Ethan; this was about her and she had to get what she needed out of it. And if that occasionally included mind-blowing sex, then so be it. She needed to get laid every so often. Ethan was more than up to the task. Casual sex in a casual marriage. No big whoop.

Ethan was waiting for her at the bar again. "Frances,"

he said, pulling her into a tight embrace and brushing his lips over her cheek. She didn't miss the way he avoided her lips. "Shall we?"

"Of course." She was ready for him tonight. He was not going to get to her.

"You're looking better," he said as he held her chair for her.

"Oh? Was I not up to your usual high standards this morning?"

Ethan's mouth quirked into a wry smile. "You seem better, too."

She waved away his backhanded compliment. "So," she said, not even bothering to look at the menu, "tell me about this mysterious Richards person. If I'm going to be accused of industrial espionage, I should at least get some of the details."

His smile froze and then fell right off his face. It made Frances feel good, the rush of power that went with catching him off guard.

So she'd had a rough night and a tough morning. She was not going down with a whimper. And if he thought he could steamroll her, well, he'd learn soon enough.

"Actually," he said, dropping his gaze to his menu, "I did want to talk to you about that. I owe you an apology."

He owed her an apology? This morning he'd accused her of betrayal. This evening—apologies?

No. She did not want to slide back into that space where he professed to care about her feelings because that was where she got into trouble. She pointedly stared at her menu.

"Do you know who Zeb Richards is?"

"No. I assume he is the Richards in question, however." She still didn't look at Ethan. She realized she was fiddling with the diamonds at her neck, but she couldn't quite help herself.

"He is." Out of the corner of her eye, she saw Ethan lay down his menu. "I don't feel it's my place to tell you this, but I don't want to come off as patronizing, so—"

"A tad late for that," she murmured in as disinterested a voice as possible.

"A company called ZOLA is trying to make my life harder. They're making noises that my company is failing at restructuring and that AllBev should sell off the Brewery. One presumes that they'll either buy it on the cheap or buy it for scrap. A company like the Brewery is worth almost as much for its parts as it is for its value."

"Indeed," she said. She managed to nail "faux sympathetic," if she did say so herself. "And this concerns me how?"

"ZOLA is run by Zeb Richards."

This time, she did put down her menu. "And…? Out with it, Ethan."

For the first time, Ethan looked unsure of himself. "Zeb Richards is your half brother."

She blinked a few times. "I have many half brothers. However, I don't particularly remember one of them being named Zeb."

"When I found out this morning that he was related to you, I assumed you were working with him."

She stared at him. "How do you know about any supposed half brothers of mine?"

"Chadwick," he added with an apologetic smile.

"I should have known," she murmured.

"I asked him if he knew about ZOLA, and he gave me a file on Richards. Including proof that you and Zeb are related."

"How very nice of him to tell *you* and not *me*." Oh, she was damnably tired of Chadwick meddling in her affairs.

"Hence why I'm trying not to be patronizing." Ethan

fiddled with his silverware. "I did not have all the facts this morning when you got to the office and I made a series of assumptions that were unfair to you."

She looked at him flatly. "Is that so? And what, pray tell, was this additional information that has apparently exonerated me so completely?"

He dropped his gaze and she knew. "Chadwick again?"

"Correct. He believes that you have never had contact with your other half brothers. So, I'm sorry about my actions this morning. I was concerned that you were working with Richards to undermine the Brewery and I know now that simply isn't the case."

This admission was probably supposed to make her feel better. It did not. "*That's* what you were concerned with? *That's* what this morning was about?"

And not her? Not the way she'd insulted him last night, the way she'd stormed out of the hotel room without even pausing long enough to get her dress zipped properly?

He'd been worried about the company. His job.

Not her.

It shouldn't hurt. After all, this entire relationship was built on the premise that he was doing it for the company. For the Brewery and for his private firm.

No, it shouldn't have hurt at all.

Funny how it did.

"I could see how you were trying to get your family identity back. It wasn't a difficult mental leap to make, you understand. But I apologize."

She stared at him. She'd wanted to get revenge. She'd wanted to bring him down several pegs and put him in his place. But she hadn't conspired with some half brother she didn't even know existed to take down the whole company.

She didn't want to take down the company. The people

who worked there were her friends, her second family. Destroying the company would be destroying them.

It'd mean destroying Ethan, too.

"You're serious. You're really apologizing?"

He nodded, the look in his eyes deepening as he leaned forward. "I should have had more faith in you. It's a mistake I won't make again."

As an apology went, it wasn't bad. Actually, it was pretty damned good. There was only one problem with it.

"So that's it? The moment things actually get messy, you assume I'm trying to ruin you. But now that my brother has confirmed that I've never even heard of Zeb Richards or whatever his name is, you're suddenly all back to 'I like you complicated, Frances'?" She scoffed and slouched away from the table.

It must have come out louder than she realized because his eyes hardened. "We are in public."

"So we are. Your point?"

A muscle in his jaw tensed. "This is the night when I ask you to marry me," he said in a low growl that, despite the war of words they were engaged in, sent a shiver down her spine because it was the exact same voice he'd used when he'd bent her over the bed and made her come. Twice.

"Is it?" she growled back. "Do you always ask women to marry you when you're losing an argument?"

He stared hard at her for a second and then, unbelievably, his lips curved into an almost smile, as if he enjoyed this. "No. But I'll make an exception for you."

"Don't," she said, suddenly afraid of this. Of him. Of what he could do to her if she let him.

"This was the deal."

"Don't," she whispered, terrified.

He pushed back from his chair in full view of everyone in the restaurant. He dropped to one knee, just like in the movies, and pulled a robin's-egg-blue box out of his pocket. "Frances," he said in a stage voice loud enough to carry across the whole space. "I know we haven't known each other very long, but I can't imagine life without you. Will you do me the honor of marrying me?"

It sounded rehearsed. It wasn't the fumbling failure at sweet nothings she'd come to expect from him. It was for show. All for show.

Just like they'd planned.

This was where the small part of her brain that wasn't freaking out—and it was a very small part—was supposed to say yes. Where she was publically supposed to declare her love for him, and they were supposed to ride off into the sunset—or, at the very least, his hotel room—and consummate their relationship. Again.

He was handsome and good in bed and a worthy opponent and rich—couldn't forget that. And he liked her most of the time. He liked her too much.

She was supposed to say yes. For the gallery. For Becky. For the Brewery, for all the workers.

She was supposed to say yes so she could make Frances Beaumont important again, so that the Beaumont name would mean what she wanted it to mean—fame and accolades and people wanting to be her friend.

She was supposed to say yes for *her*. This was what she wanted.

Wasn't it?

Ethan's face froze. "Well?" he demanded in a quiet voice. "Frances."

Say yes, her brain urged. *Say yes right now.*

"I…" She was horrified to hear her voice come out as a whisper. "I can't."

His eyes widened in horror or confusion or some unholy mix of the two, she didn't know. She didn't wait around to find out. She bolted out of the restaurant as fast as she could in her heels. She didn't even wait to get her coat.

She ran. It was an act of cowardice. An act of surrender.

She'd ceded the game.

She'd lost everything.

Sixteen

"Frances?"

What the hell just happened? One second, he was following the script because, yes, he damn well had planned out the proposal. It was for public consumption.

The next second, she was gone, cutting an emerald-green swath through the suddenly silent restaurant.

"Frances, wait!" he called out, painfully aware that this was not part of the plan. He lunged to his feet and took off after her. She couldn't just leave—not like that. This wasn't how it was supposed to go.

Okay, today had not been his best work. He'd acted without all the available facts this morning and clearly, that had been a bad move. There were no such things as coincidences—except, it seemed, for right now.

Yes, he should have given her the benefit of the doubt and yes, he probably should have groveled a little more. The relief Ethan had felt when Chadwick had told him the only Beaumonts who knew of Zeb's identity were him and Matthew had been no small thing. Frances hadn't been plotting to overthrow the company. In fact, she'd been apologizing to Ethan. They could reset at dinner and continue on as they had been.

But he hadn't expected her to run away from him—especially not after the way she'd dressed him down after they'd had sex.

If she didn't want to get married, he thought as he gave chase, why the hell hadn't she just said so? He'd given her an out—several outs. And she'd refused his concessions at every turn, only to leave him hanging with a diamond engagement ring in his hand.

This wasn't right, damn it.

He caught up with her trying to hail a cab. He could see her shivering in the cold wind. "For God's sake, Frances," he said, shucking his suit jacket and slinging it around her shoulders. "You'll catch your death."

"Ethan," she said in the most plaintive voice he'd ever heard.

"What are you doing?" he demanded. "This was the deal."

"I know, I know…" She didn't elucidate on that knowledge, however.

"Frances." He took her by the arm and pulled her a step back from the curb. "We agreed—we agreed this *morning*—that I was going to ask you to marry me and you were going to say yes." When she didn't look at him, he dropped her arm and cupped her face in his hands. "Babe, talk to me."

"Don't *babe* me, Ethan."

"Then talk, damn it. What the hell happened?"

"I—I can't. I thought I could, but I can't. Don't you see?" He shook his head. "I thought—I thought I didn't need love. That I could do this and it'd be no different than watching my parents fight, no different than all the other men who wanted to get close to the Beaumont name and money. You weren't supposed to be *different*, Ethan. You were supposed to be the *same*."

Then, as he watched in horror, a tear slipped past her blinking eyelid and began to trickle down her cheek.

"I wasn't supposed to like you. And you, you big idiot, you weren't supposed to like me," she said, her voice quiet and shaky as more tears followed the first.

He tried to wipe the tears away with his thumb, but they were replaced too quickly. "I don't understand how liking each other makes marrying each other a bad thing," he said.

"You're here for your company. You're not here for me," she said, cutting him off before he could protest.

An unfamiliar feeling began to push past the confusion and the frustration—a feeling that he hadn't often allowed himself to feel.

Panic.

And he wasn't sure why. It could be that, if the workers at the Brewery got it in their collective heads that he'd broken their Frannie's heart, they might draw and quarter him. He could be panicking that his foolproof method of regaining control over his business felt suddenly very foolish.

But that wasn't it. That wasn't it at all.

"See?" She sniffed. She was openly crying at this point. It was horrifying because as much as she might have berated him for being lousy at the game when he dared admit that he might have feelings for her, he knew this was not a play on her part. "How long will it last?"

His mouth opened. *A year*, he almost said, because that was the deal.

"I could love you," he told her and it was God's honest truth. "If you'll let me."

Her eyes closed, and she turned her head away. "Ethan…" she whispered, so softly he almost didn't hear it over the sound of a cab pulling up next to them. "I could love you, too." For a moment, he thought she was agreeing; she was seeing the light, and they'd get in the cab and carry on as planned.

But then she added, "I won't settle for *could*. Not anymore. I can't believe I'm saying this, but I want to be in love with the man I marry. And I want him to be in love with me, too. I want to believe I'm worth that—worth something more than a business deal. Worth more than some company."

"You are," he said, but it didn't sound convincing, not even to his own ears. "You *are*, Frances."

She gave him a sad smile full of heartache. "I want to believe that, Ethan. But I'm not a prize to be won in the game. Not anymore."

She slipped his jacket off her slim shoulders and held it out to him.

He didn't want to take it. He didn't want her to go. "Keep it. I don't want you to freeze."

She shook her head no, and the cabbie honked and shouted, "Lady, you need a ride or not?" so Frances ducked into the cab.

He stood there, freezing his ass off as he watched the cab's taillights disappear down the street.

When he'd talked to Chadwick Beaumont on the phone today, he'd barely been able to wait for Chadwick to get done explaining who the hell Zeb Richards was before asking, "Does Frances know about this?" because he'd been desperate to know if she was leading him on or if those moments he'd thought where honesty were real.

"Unless she's hired her own private investigators, the only people who know about my father's illegitimate children are me and Matthew. My mother was the one who originally tracked down the oldest three. She'd long suspected my father was cheating on her," he had added. "There are others."

"And you don't think Frances would have hired her own PI?"

"Problem?" Chadwick had said in such a genial way that

Ethan had almost confided in him that he might have just accused Chadwick's younger sister of industrial espionage.

"No," Ethan had said because, at the time, it hadn't been a problem. A little lover's quarrel, nothing that a thirty-thousand-dollar diamond ring couldn't fix. "Just trying to understand the Beaumont family tree."

"Good luck with that," was all Chadwick had said.

Ethan had thanked him for the information and promised to pass along anything new he learned. Then he'd eaten his donuts and thought about how he'd make it up to Frances.

She'd promised not to love him—not to even like him. She'd told him to do the same. He should have listened to her, but he hadn't lied. When it came to her, he couldn't quite help himself. Everything about her had been an impulse. Even his original proposal had been half impulse, driven by some basic desire to outwit Frances Beaumont.

Their entire relationship had been based on a game of one-upmanship. In that regard, she'd gotten the final word. She'd said no.

Well, hell. Now what? He'd publically proposed, been publically rejected and his whole plan had fallen apart on him. And the worst thing was that he wasn't sure *why*. Was it because he hadn't trusted her this morning when she'd said she didn't know anything about Richards?

Or was it because, despite it all, he did like her? He liked her a great deal. More than was wise, that much was sure.

This morning she'd shown up at his office with the donuts he'd requested. She hadn't had on a stitch of her armor—no designer clothes, no impenetrable attitude. She'd been a woman who'd sat down, admitted fault and apologized for her actions.

She'd been trying to show him that she liked him. Enough to be honest with him.

He'd thrown that trust back in her face. And then cavalierly assumed that a big rock was going to make it up to her.

Idiot. She wanted to know she was worth it—and she hadn't meant worth diamonds and roses.

He was in too deep to let her go. She *was* worth it.

So this was what falling in love was like.

How was he going to convince her that this wasn't part of the game?

Frances was not surprised when no extravagant floral arrangement arrived the next day. No chocolates or champagne or jewels showed up, either.

They didn't arrive the day after that. Or the third, for that matter.

And why would they? She was not bound to Ethan. She had no claim on him, nor he on her. The only thing that remained of their failed, doomed "relationship" were several vases of withering flowers and an expensive necklace.

She had taken off the necklace.

But she hadn't been able to bring herself to return it. Not to him, not to the store for cash—cash she could use, now that the gallery was dead and she had no other job prospects, aside from selling her family's heirlooms on the open market.

The necklace sat on her bedside table, mocking her as she went to sleep every night.

She called Becky but didn't feel like talking except to say, "The funding is probably not going to happen, so plan accordingly."

To which Becky had replied, "We'll get it figured out, one way or the other."

That was the sort of platitude people said when the situation was hopeless but they needed to feel better. So Frances had replied, "Sure, we'll get together for lunch soon and go over our options," because that was the sort of thing rational grown-ups said all the time.

Then she'd ended the call and crawled back under the covers.

Byron had texted, but what could she tell him? That she'd done the not-rash thing for the first time in her life and was now miserable? And why, exactly, was she miserable again? She shouldn't be hiding under the covers in her cozy jammies! She'd won! She'd stopped Ethan in his tracks with a move he couldn't anticipate and he couldn't recover from. She'd brought him firmly down to where he belonged. He wasn't good enough for the Beaumonts, and he wasn't good enough for the Brewery.

Victory was hers!

She didn't think victory was supposed to taste this sour.

She didn't believe in love. Never had, never would. So why, when the next best thing had presented itself—someone who was fond of her, who admired her, and who could still make her shiver with need, someone who had offered to generously provide for her financial future in exchange for a year of her life even—*why* had she walked away?

Because he was only here for the company. And, fool that she was, she'd suddenly realized she wanted someone who was going to be here for her.

"I could love you." She heard his words over and over again, beating against her brain like a spike. He could.

But he didn't.

What a mess.

Luckily, she was used to it.

She'd managed to drag herself to the shower on the fourth day. She had decided that she was going to stop moping. Moping didn't get jobs, and it didn't heal broken hearts. She needed to get up and, at the very least, have lunch with Becky or go see Byron. She needed to do something that would eventually get her out of the Beaumont mansion because she was *done* living under the same roof as Chadwick. She was going to tell him that the very next time she saw him, too.

She'd just buttoned her jeans when she heard the doorbell. She ignored it as she toweled her hair.

Then someone knocked on her bedroom door. "Frannie?" It was Serena, Chadwick's wife. "Flowers for you."

"Really?" Who would send her flowers? Not Ethan. Not at this late date. "Hang on." She threw on a sweater and opened the door.

Serena stood there, an odd look on her face. She was not holding any flowers. "Um… I think you need to get these yourself," Serena said before she turned and walked down the hall.

Frances stood there, all the warning bells going off in her head at once.

Her heart pounding, she walked down the hallway and peered over the edge of the railing. There, in the middle of the foyer, stood Ethan, holding a single red rose.

She must have made a noise or gasped or something because he looked up at her and smiled. A good smile, the kind of smile that made her want to do something ridiculous like kiss him when she absolutely should not be glad to see him at all.

She needed to say something witty and urbane and snarky that would put him in his place, so that for at least a minute, she could feel like Frances Beaumont again.

Instead, she said, "You're here."

Damn. Worse, it came out breathy, as if she couldn't believe he'd actually ventured into the lair of the Beaumonts.

"I am," he replied, his gaze never leaving her face. "I came for you."

Oh. That was terribly close to a sweet nothing—no, it

wasn't a nothing. It was a sweet something. But what? "I'm here. I've been here for a few days now."

There, that was a good thing to say. Something that let him know that his apology—if this even was an apology—was days late and, judging by the single flower he was holding, dollars short.

"I had some things to do," he said. "Can you come down here?"

"Why should I?"

His grin spread. "Because I don't want to shout? But I will." He cleared his throat. *"Frances!"* he shouted, his voice ringing off the marble and the high-vaulted ceilings. *"Can you come down here? Please?"*

"Okay, okay!" She didn't know who else besides Serena was home, but she didn't need to have Ethan yelling at the top of his lungs.

She hurried down the wide staircase with Ethan watching her the entire time. She slowed only when she got to the last few steps. She didn't want to be on his level, not just yet. "I'm here," she said again.

He held out the lone red rose to her. "I brought you a flower."

"Just one?"

"One seemed…fitting, somehow." He looked her over. "How have you been?"

"Oh, fine," she tried to say lightly. "Just hanging out around the house, trying to avoid social media and gossip columns—the normal stuff, really. Just another day in the life of a Beaumont."

He took a step closer to her. It made her tense. "You don't have to do that," he said, his voice soft and quiet and just for her.

"Do what?"

"Put your armor on. I didn't come here looking for a fight."

She eyed him warily. What was this? A single rose? A claim that he didn't want to fight? "Then why did you come?"

He took another step in—close enough to touch her. Which he did. He lifted his hand and brushed his fingertips down her cheek. "I wanted to tell you that you're worth it."

She froze under his touch, the rose between them. "We aren't in public, Ethan. You don't have to do this. It's over. We made a scene. It's fine. We can go on with our lives now." Her words came out in a rush.

"Do you really believe that? That it's fine?"

"Isn't it?" Her voice cracked, damn it.

"It isn't. Three days without you has almost driven me mad."

"I drive you mad when we're together. I drive you mad when we're apart—you know how to make a woman feel special." The words should have sounded flippant. They didn't. No matter how hard she tried, she couldn't convince herself that this was no big deal. Not when Ethan was staring into her eyes with this odd look of satisfaction on his face, not when his thumb was now stroking her cheek.

"Why are you here?" she whispered, desperate to hear the answer and just as desperate to not hear it.

"I came for you. I've never met anyone like you before, and I don't want to walk away from you. Not now, not ever."

"It's all just talk, Ethan." Her voice was the barest of whispers. She was doing a lousy job convincing herself. She didn't think she was convincing him at all.

"Do you know how much you're worth to me?"

She shook her head. "Some diamonds, some flowers. A rose."

He stepped in another bit, bringing her body almost into contact with his. "As of yesterday, I am no longer the CEO of the Beaumont Brewery."

"What?"

"I quit the job. For personal reasons. My second in command, Finn Jackson, flew in today to take over the restructuring project. We're still dealing with a little fallout from AllBev, but it's nothing I can't handle." He said it as if it were just a little speed bump.

"You *quit*? The Brewery?"

"It wasn't my company. It wasn't worth it to me. Not like you are."

"I don't understand." He was saying words that she understood individually. But the way he was stringing them together? It didn't make sense. Not a bit.

Something in his eyes changed—deepened. A small shiver ran down Frances's back. "I do not need to marry you to solidify my position within the company because I no longer work for the company. I do not need to worry about unknown relations trying to overthrow my position because I have given up the position. The company was never worth more than you were."

She blinked at him. All of her words failed her. She had nothing to hide behind now.

"So," he went on, his eyes full of honesty and sincerity and hope. All of those things she hadn't believed she deserved. "Here I am. I have quit the Brewery. I have taken a leave of absence from my company. I could care less if anyone's listening to what we say or watching how we say it. All I care about is you. Even when you're messy and complicated and even when I say the wrong thing at the wrong time, I care about *you*."

"You can't mean that," she whispered, because what if he did?

"I can and I do. I truly never believed I would meet anyone I could care about, much less someone who would mean more to me than the job. But I did. It's you, Frances. I want you when your armor's up because you make sarcasm and irony into high art. I want you when you're feeling vulnerable and honest because I want to be that soft place where you can land after a hard day of putting the world in its place. And I want you all the times in between, when you challenge me and call me on my mistakes and push me to be a better man—one who can keep up with you."

Unexpectedly, he dropped to his knees. "So I'm asking you again. Not for the Brewery, not for the employees, not for the public. I'm asking you for me. Because I want to spend my life with you. Not a few months, not a year—my life. Our lives. Together."

"You want to marry me? *Me?*"

"I like you," he said simply. "I shouldn't, but I do. Even worse, I love you." He gave her a crooked grin. "I love you. I'd recommend you love me, too."

Her mouth opened, but nothing came out. Not a damn thing. Because what was she going to say? That he'd gotten better at sweet nothings? That he was crazy to have fallen for her? That…

That she wanted to say yes—but she was afraid?

"I've seen the real you," he said, still on his knees. "And that's the woman I love."

"Do we get—married? Next week?" That had been the deal, hadn't it? A whirlwind courtship, married in two weeks.

"I'm not making a deal, Frances. All I'm doing right now is asking a simple question. We can wait a year, if you want. You're worth the wait. I'm not going anywhere without you."

"It won't ever be simple," she warned him. "I don't have it in me."

He stood and pulled her into his arms as if she'd said yes, when she wasn't sure she had yet. The rose, she feared, was a total loss. "I don't want you simple. I want to know that every day, I've fought for you and every day, you've chosen me again."

Was it possible, what he was saying? Could a man love her?

"I expect to be wined and dined and courted," she warned him, trying to sound stern and mostly just laughing.

He laughed with her. "And what do I get out of this again?"

"A wife. A messy, complicated wife who will love you until the end of time."

"Perfect," he said, lowering his lips to hers. "That's *exactly* what I wanted."

* * * * *

If you loved Frances's story,
pick up the first four books in the
BEAUMONT HEIRS *series:*

NOT THE BOSS'S BABY
TEMPTED BY A COWBOY
A BEAUMONT CHRISTMAS WEDDING
HIS SON, HER SECRET

Available now from Harlequin Desire!

If you're on Twitter, tell us what you think of
Harlequin Desire! #harlequindesire

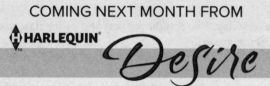

REQUEST YOUR FREE BOOKS!

2 FREE NOVELS PLUS 2 FREE GIFTS!

HARLEQUIN®

Desire

ALWAYS POWERFUL, PASSIONATE AND PROVOCATIVE

YES! Please send me 2 FREE Harlequin® Desire novels and my 2 FREE gifts (gifts are worth about $10). After receiving them, if I don't wish to receive any more books, I can return the shipping statement marked "cancel." If I don't cancel, I will receive 6 brand-new novels every month and be billed just $4.55 per book in the U.S. or $5.24 per book in Canada. That's a savings of at least 13% off the cover price! It's quite a bargain! Shipping and handling is just 50¢ per book in the U.S. and 75¢ per book in Canada.* I understand that accepting the 2 free books and gifts places me under no obligation to buy anything. I can always return a shipment and cancel at any time. Even if I never buy another book, the two free books and gifts are mine to keep forever.

225/326 HDN GH2P

Name _____ (PLEASE PRINT)

Address _____ Apt. #

City _____ State/Prov. _____ Zip/Postal Code

Signature (if under 18, a parent or guardian must sign)

Mail to the **Reader Service:**

IN U.S.A.: P.O. Box 1867, Buffalo, NY 14240-1867
IN CANADA: P.O. Box 609, Fort Erie, Ontario L2A 5X3

Want to try two free books from another line?
Call 1-800-873-8635 or visit www.ReaderService.com.

* Terms and prices subject to change without notice. Prices do not include applicable taxes. Sales tax applicable in N.Y. Canadian residents will be charged applicable taxes. Offer not valid in Quebec. This offer is limited to one order per household. Not valid for current subscribers to Harlequin Desire books. All orders subject to credit approval. Credit or debit balances in a customer's account(s) may be offset by any other outstanding balance owed by or to the customer. Please allow 4 to 6 weeks for delivery. Offer available while quantities last.

Your Privacy—The Reader Service is committed to protecting your privacy. Our Privacy Policy is available online at www.ReaderService.com or upon request from the Reader Service.

We make a portion of our mailing list available to reputable third parties that offer products we believe may interest you. If you prefer that we not exchange your name with third parties, or if you wish to clarify or modify your communication preferences, please visit us at www.ReaderService.com/consumerchoice or write to us at Reader Service Preference Service, P.O. Box 9062, Buffalo, NY 14240-9062. Include your complete name and address.

HD15

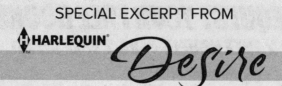
Bailey wondered what there was about Walker that was
different from any other man. All it took was the feel of
his hand on her shoulder... His touch affected her in a
way no man's touch had ever affected her before. How did
he have the ability to breach her inner being and remind
her that she was a woman?

Personal relationships weren't her forte. Most of the
guys in these parts were too afraid of her brothers and
cousins to even think of crossing the line, so she'd only
had one lover in her lifetime. And for her it had been
one and done, and executed more out of curiosity than
anything else. She certainly hadn't been driven by any
type of sexual desire like she felt for Walker.

There was this spike of heat that always rolled in her
stomach whenever she was around him, not to mention
a warmth that would settle in the area between her legs.

Even now, just being in the same vehicle with him was making her breasts tingle. Was she imagining things or had his face inched a little closer to hers?

Suggesting they go for a late-night ride might not have been a good idea, after all. "I'm not perfect," she finally said softly.

"No one is perfect," he responded huskily.

Bailey drew in a sharp breath when he reached up and rubbed a finger across her cheek. She fought back the slow moan that threatened to slip past her lips. His hand on her shoulder had caused internal havoc, and now his fingers on her face were stirring something to life inside her that she'd never felt before.

She needed to bring an end to this madness. The last thing she wanted was for him to get the wrong idea about the reason she'd brought him here. "I didn't bring you out here for this, Walker," she said. "I don't want you getting the wrong idea."

"Okay, what's the right idea?" he asked, leaning in even closer. "Why did you bring me out here?"

Nervously, she licked her lips. He was still rubbing a finger across her cheek. "To apologize."

He lowered his head and took possession of her mouth.

Don't miss
BREAKING BAILEY'S RULES
by New York Times *bestselling author*
Brenda Jackson, available November 2015 wherever
Harlequin® Desire books and ebooks are sold.

www.Harlequin.com

THE WORLD IS BETTER WITH

Romance

Harlequin has everything from contemporary, passionate and heartwarming to suspenseful and inspirational stories.

Whatever your mood, we have a romance just for you!

Connect with us to find your next great read, special offers and more.

f /HarlequinBooks

🐦 @HarlequinBooks

www.HarlequinBlog.com

www.Harlequin.com/Newsletters

◆ HARLEQUIN®

A *Romance* FOR EVERY MOOD™

www.Harlequin.com